Suleiman the Artist

Suleiman the Artist

Published by The Conrad Press Ltd. in the United Kingdom 2023

Tel: +44(0)1227 472 874

www.theconradpress.com
info@theconradpress.com

ISBN 978-1-915494-92-4

Copyright © Carol Shimell-Haines 2023
All rights reserved.

Typesetting and cover design by Michelle Emerson
www.michelleemerson.co.uk

The Conrad Press logo was designed by Maria Priestley

Printed and bound in Great Britain by Clays Ltd, Elcograf S.p.A.

Suleiman the Artist

Carol Shimell-Haines

Pour Mélanie et Nicolas

To
My husband, Tom.
Thank you for believing in me and for your endless patience.

And
To my enthusiastic group of friends…
Thank you for your constant support and encouragement.
Geneviève, Jill, June, Pam
And Liz.

Chapter 1

Yusuf Abadi, the distinguished violinist, a man whose talents had been compared to that of the great Yehudi Menuhin, a man of such wealth he could command anything at his slightest whim, was so full of rage he wanted to shake his fists at the heavens and scream to a God that he no longer believed in...

Breathing deeply and crushing his anger, that same great violinist sat on the wide bed gently cradling his wife in his arms, whispering in her ear that he loved her and would always love only her.

Through the open windows, he could hear the idle chatter of their two little daughters playing together in the warm sunshine. Hearing them so happy made him forget – but only for one brief intake of breath - the sadness that was squeezing his heart.

A slight breeze caused the white, cotton curtains to flutter and billow creating a sudden flow of cool air.

'Elena,' he whispered. 'Our new baby girl is very beautiful.'

As he spoke, the final warmth of the afternoon sun slipped silently into the bedroom, settling on the silk sheet that covered his wife's exhausted body.

She raised dull grey eyes to look at him in silence.

He saw no smile on her pale lips.

'Another daughter. Forgive me, Yusuf.' Her voice was faint.

He thought: three daughters in so many years... He refused to count Elena's first born, the unmentionable one, the secret one. The one that would have brought shame to the family - and the count up to four.

He felt her slipping away and he was afraid.

'Elena, please, hold on. Hold on to me. You will get stronger. I promise you. The doctors...' his voice trailed away. He wanted to reassure her but he could not: there was nothing to be done.

The doctors had told him: *She must have no more children: it would be fatal.*

He lowered his head. He should have listened; he should have forced his wife to listen. He turned his face towards the window so she would not see his dark eyes wet with the tears he held back.

'Shall I ask the nursemaid to bring the baby to you?' he asked.

She shook her head, her hair still thick and black as a raven's wing spread across the pillow. She repressed a sob.

He thought: it is the pain.

A wave of panic rose up in his chest. She was too young, too young to die. Why couldn't he make the pain go away?

He felt the light touch of her fingers on his arm.

She said, 'I am tired, Yusuf. So very tired.'

He prayed silently to God to bring her back to him,

bring her back to life. But he knew that God was not listening.

He said, 'Do you remember when I asked your father's permission to marry you? He told me that you were his favourite daughter and that he would never part with you. He said I was too old, but I told him my friends said that I carried my years well and that had made him laugh.'

She said, 'You promised him you would build me a palace.'

'Did I keep that promise?'

'Yusuf, you built me more than a palace.' She stopped.

He was so afraid that if he stopped speaking, if she closed her eyes...

'And our wedding day - we were so happy, weren't we? You do remember?'

Perhaps the memories of that day, not so long ago, would keep her with him.

He said, 'When I reached the wedding hall and you were standing there, ready to welcome me, I could not speak. I almost lost my voice! You looked...' he shook his head because he could not find the right words. 'You looked... radiant. I could not believe that you were to become my wife. That was the happiest day of my life – have I ever told you?'

If he closed his eyes now, which he dared not, he would be able to see her as she had been then: tall and slender as a willow, dressed in a wedding gown of white lace; her dark, luxuriant hair piled high upon her head. He would once again see her wide mouth and generous smile, and her eyes, 'the colour of the sky on a rainy day,' he had once told her. She had laughed.

He said, 'Do you remember the flowers on our wedding day? They were everywhere - their perfume was intoxicating! Some guests even complained of headaches! And the food! It was amazing, heavenly! Everyone said so.' He continued to speak, he could not stop. 'And there was so much laughter. So much happiness. And how we danced! You and I. My new and beautiful wife.'

She lifted a slim hand to reach out and stroke his dark beard, a white diamond ring now too loose on her finger.

'And you my husband, so handsome. All my friends were jealous. You played your violin. For me. Only for me.'

He pressed his ear nearer to hear her whispered words. 'You played our favourite music.'

He put a hand over his eyes: the tears must wait.

'Yes, for you, just for you. I played the Russian waltz. And you danced with your father.'

He offered up a silent prayer to the heavens. 'Forgive me if I have caused offence. I have already been punished once. Do not punish me again. Please do not take her away. Please let her stay with me a while longer. I am begging you. Please, please let Elena live.'

Before their wedding, and as he had promised her father, Yusuf ordered a magnificent house to be built for his future wife, with large, airy rooms and high ceilings. As you entered the house, two wide, marble staircases greeted you on either side of the entrance hall. There was a ballroom where orchestras entertained and people danced - and where he would play his violin.

He placed paintings of great men astride white stallions on the high walls and, in hidden corners, cool fountains sprung out of blue and gold mosaic floors.

He said to his gardener, 'Moonif, I have visions of a walled garden with beautiful, perfumed flowers and lemon and olive groves. I want you to create such a garden for me. There should also be a pool of cool, clear water where my wife and I shall bathe, away from prying eyes.'

And then he said, 'I want this garden to be of such beauty that even Allah will be jealous!'

He remembered those last words because he remembered how Moonif had taken a step back and stared at him, shocked at the blasphemy.

But he had meant no harm. It had all been for Elena, only for Elena.

Now, as he kissed Elena's forehead, it felt moist, clammy.

'We shall dance again, you and I.' he whispered fiercely to her, his voice breaking.

'*Inshallah*. Do not be angry, Yusuf. We cannot fight fate.'

He held her closer, kissing her cold cheek.

He wanted to hold his head in his hands and weep as he continued to send up silent prayers to the God he had offended, recalling the events of that terrible day, several months after they had returned home from their honeymoon.

It had been a day of intense heat, when the whole world had fallen silent: no bird song, no rustling of a cool breeze in the branches of the olive and lemon trees.

'Yusuf, it's so hot. I think I shall go and bathe in our pool. Why don't you come with me?' Elena had asked him, enticing him with her grey, almond-shaped eyes and long black lashes.

He had smiled and kissed her cheek. 'Later.' He whispered in her ear. 'I have work to prepare.'

He had returned to his music room and stood by the open window, playing the Russian waltz by Shostakovich.

He had played to the heavens.

He believed that to play music meant he was closer to heaven.

Today, he bowed his head in shame at his arrogance.

And Elena had gone to bathe alone, her long dark hair tumbling down her naked back.

And while he played the violin, the notes of that waltz floated out and up into the heavens, and a stranger climbed over the high wall that surrounded the garden.

The stranger crept stealthily out of the shadows.

He went down to the pool where Elena was bathing. Placing a filthy hand over her mouth, he dragged her out of the water and threw her down onto the hard ground where he forced himself into her, taking possession of every part of her body.

It was a moment that Yusuf did not witness, but it was a moment that produced a nightmare that would play in his head over and over again until the day of his death.

Later, when he had finished rehearsing his concert pieces, Yusuf went down to the pool where he found his wife, sobbing and broken, curled into a tight ball as she tried to hide herself away.

When he saw her, and to his shame, he turned away to vomit.

Too late, he ran over to the high wall, howling with rage, murder in his mind, but he found no-one, nothing. Only a few broken branches lying on the ground.

He carried Elena's injured, bruised body through that beautiful garden with the exotic flowers, back into the palace he had built for her.

He carried her up the wide, marble staircase, past the proud riders astride their stallions, through the elegant rooms, and in his arms she weighed no more than the lightest feather.

Then Elena begged him to close and lock all the doors, refusing to see a doctor or a nurse.

And so he bathed her, comforted her, loved her, and brought her back to life.

Nine months later, the fruit of that shocking day entered the world silently, perhaps already aware of the secrecy: small legs and hands that kicked, rosy lips and grey eyes that searched for a love that was not there.

He recalled his silent fury, how he had wanted to smother the living, breathing 'thing' that lay beside his wife.

Elena had held the boy one brief moment before he was taken from her, but not before she had taken a small lock of his hair.

Yusuf summoned a holy man. 'Take the child. Get rid of it. I never want to see nor hear of it ever again.' There had been venom in his voice. 'Do you understand? Here is money. Take it away.'

'Yusuf,' her whispered voice broke into his thoughts.

'I am here, my dearest.'

'Promise me you will take care of our daughters.'

He nodded because he did not trust himself to speak.

She seemed satisfied as she said, 'Play our music, please Yusuf.'

Gently, he lay her back down on the bed.

He walked over to the window and stood staring out, recalling the joyous times when they had travelled together, when they had been deliriously happy with a happiness that only comes with pure love.

All was now quiet. Peaceful. The children had gone inside. The sun was beginning to set a deep red.

In the far distance he could see the snow-capped mountains, a river that snaked its way across the valley to the village that lay on the other side and he realized with great sadness that not a single person in the whole world was aware of how, at this precise moment, his life was collapsing.

He picked up the violin and went back to sit near Elena.

As he played, tears slipped down his face.

These days there was a guilt that lurked in the shadows, goading him, asking him over and over, what if he had kept the child?

Would God be looking on him more kindly today?

Would God be willing to spare him his beloved wife?

He saw her close her eyes and breathe a deep sigh.

As he pulled the bow over the strings, and as the sounds went higher and higher, he knew that he would never again play to God.

He barely heard her last words to him, barely heard her question.

'Did you give my son a name?'

She was gone before he could say, 'I named him Suleiman.'

Chapter 2

Some twenty years after these events, Anthony J. Nicholson – or Tony to his friends, of which there were few - sat in the office of the London-based art magazine *International Horizons*.

He took a gulp out of a mug of hot, sweet coffee before replacing it on the table beside him. He shifted his bulky frame on the uncomfortable office chair, suppressing an irritable sigh.

He needed to make an urgent call to his bookie. He intended to place a fairly large bet on a race that afternoon, working on that time-worn saying: *If at first you don't succeed....*

'How long have you been working with us, Tony?'

Tony looked down at the thick pile of the gold and navy carpet with its geometrical design. He wanted to say, 'Frankly speaking, Simon, too long.' He didn't. 'Just over three years, I'm guessing.'

To be fair, he knew exactly how long he'd been working for Simon; he could even have pinpointed the actual day, if asked.

It had been late in the afternoon and he'd just come out of the bookmakers. He'd been heading for the pub next door to drown his catastrophic run of bad luck...

'Say! Is it you, Tony?'

He'd been somewhat taken aback at seeing Simon standing there: the same blue eyes, the same chestnut hair falling across his forehead, the same rosy cheeks and asinine smile he remembered from Art College.

'You haven't changed one bit! This is amazing! How are you?' Simon put out a hand and patted Tony on the shoulder. 'It's great to see you!'

It took Tony a few moments to gather his thoughts: losing a large sum of money a few minutes previously had thrown him somewhat off kilter. Now, being accosted by a man he had always held in contempt, seemed the culmination of an extremely bad day.

Simon, however, continued to babble along as if it were only yesterday they had been at Art College together.

'It must be all of twenty odd years! Fancy bumping into you! There's a pub just next door. What about a catch up?'

Tony caught a whiff of an expensive aftershave as he took in Simon's bespoke suit and fancy shoes.

'Why not,' he said.

When Simon had finished explaining how he was owner, and editor, of a London based art magazine and how business was booming; that he had a beautiful wife, three kids at private school and a villa in the south of France, Tony's brain began to work energetically.

When Simon finally asked over a glass of cold lager, 'How about you?' he was ready...

After leaving Art College and finding himself unemployed with no prospects in sight, Tony explained how he'd gone on a short course in journalism. He'd obtained excellent grades and after several mundane jobs, finally managed to get a post as a reporter with a London tabloid.

'Sounds like you landed on your feet.'

'Well it was tough to start with, Simon, and I didn't have any family money behind me, of course.' The disparaging, but true comment went unnoticed. 'I've done reasonably well. Pay's been good, the odd perks, you know...'

'I always knew you'd be a success, Tony.' Simon grinned widely.

Tony swallowed hard: he'd always found Simon patronising, with his arrogant airs, and the way he threw his money around.

'Unfortunately, Simon,' he looked away, 'I've just been made redundant. This morning, in fact.'

He stopped and looked down at his shoes, twisting his mouth as his lips formed the lie: the truth was, he'd handed in his notice a few months back, when he'd come into an unexpected and sizeable amount of money.

Regrettably, his gambling habit had led him down a path that had gone disastrously wrong, and that afternoon he had finally lost the lot.

'Redundant? That's bad luck. What happened?'

'Simple. I was told the paper had to make cut backs due to failing business, and I happened to be one of those cut backs. So here I am, on the redundant scrap heap.' He paused. 'It came as a bit of a shock,' he said. 'Years I've been working my arse off at that paper, and here I am. A statistic.'

He shook his head despondently, picked up his glass of lager and emptied it.

'That is serious bad luck, Tony. I'm really sorry. Here, let me get you another.' Simon reached out to take his glass. 'Then let's have a chat. I think I have an idea.'

'Could you make it a double brandy?'

And now, here he was, an employee of Mr Simon Thornby, the editor and owner of *International Horizons*.

An employee with an expensive gambling habit that needed to be fed at regular intervals.

'I'd really appreciate it Tony, if you'd consider going out there.'

Tony shifted his gaze to the map Simon had spread out across his desk. He said, 'I'd rather you sent somebody else.'

'Come on, we both know you're my best journalist for this job. You've got a good eye - and a good nose for sniffing out snippets of hidden information.'

Tony ignored the flattery: he'd used that approach too many times himself.

Simon waved enthusiastically at the framed front covers that lined the walls of his office. On each front cover of *International Horizons* was a short list of the articles contained within.

'Think of the headline, *Art correspondent uncovers hidden secret behind success of talented artist.* Simon tapped his finger on the map, identifying a country torn apart by warring factions over recent years.

'What do you say? I'd make it worth your while. This artist, Suleiman bin Abadi, we know practically nothing about him, only that he was young, incredibly gifted and that he came from somewhere around here.'

This time, Simon's finger pointed to a small area on the map, the name of which was too small to read without a magnifying glass. 'I think he deserves some sort of recognition. I like the sound of him. He was young, talented. How'd he get to Europe? When? I'm sure our readers would love to hear his story.'

Tony bit his bottom lip. He had no intention of going to that godforsaken place. 'Get real, Simon! He was gifted, I grant you that, but you'd be wasting your time – and mine. He was just another illegal who struck lucky: right time, right place. What else is there to add?'

'I get that, but what happened to him? He was on the verge of becoming one of the most sort after artists on the planet! I don't understand.' Simon pushed his glasses back on top of his head. 'Apparently, he exhibited most of his work at an art gallery in Paris.'

Tony crossed his legs. 'In which case, wouldn't it be easier if I just went over to Paris and visited the gallery?'

'I'd already thought of that. I spoke to the guy who owns the place, a Jean-Louis Barre. He said he couldn't help, and that Suleiman Abadi always clammed up whenever he was asked about his past.'

'Simon, these people – these migrants, refugees, whatever you want to call them – most are hiding something pretty unpalatable. Something they don't want us to know about.'

Tony picked up the mug of coffee and drained it of its contents. He was desperate for a cigarette. 'Besides, the war out there's been going on for the best part of ten years. I doubt there's anything left to find out. People will have moved on...'

'Go out there, Tony. Please. Get people to talk to you. See what you can uncover... Why'd he leave? How did he end up in Paris?'

Tony avoided the temptation to glance down at his watch and instead stared across at one of the wide office windows that gave onto the London traffic below. 'It's all about money, you know.' He looked back at Simon.

'Think of it as a challenge, Tony! Detective work! I've had a word with my contact at the Foreign Office. It's quietened down a lot over there, and they've given us the okay, as long as you've got all the necessary paperwork and you're careful and don't go reporting on anything political. Besides, you'd be doing me a personal favour.' He paused, looked straight at Tony. 'And I'd make sure you were well rewarded.'

Tony sighed and sat back. Resting his elbows on the arms of the chair he put up his hands so the tips of his plump fingers touched, closed his lips tightly and ran his tongue around his mouth.

He turned his eyes back to the table and the map and debated inwardly for a few moments...

There seemed little point in informing Simon that he had already met Suleiman bin Abadi, while he was still working for the London tabloid.

He'd had a call one morning.

'Tony! There's been a fire at a refugee camp just outside Calais. I need you to go over there and get me a story. I need some dramatic headlines!' His boss had shouted excitedly down the phone. 'I'll make sure you get a decent bonus!"

It had been sometime in late March, early April. He couldn't remember precisely, but he did remember how cold it had felt when he arrived at the port of Calais. There was a raw wind that, literally, bit into your face.

When he finally reached the camp there were police patrols everywhere, their vans parked outside as they shouted and struggled to round up refugees into groups that scattered and reformed as the dispossessed moved about, or huddled together in silent anger, waiting for buses to carry them away to some other unknown destination.

Some were crying, some were calling out for missing friends or family.

He saw a fire engine parked outside, the fire fighters were clearing up, ready to leave.

Someone said that at least one person had been burnt to death.

A woman raised an empty palm in his direction: a waste of time.

Inside what had once been 'tent city' burnt debris of cardboard and partially melted plastic flew about.

He saw what was left of a child's jacket, a solitary, abandoned shoe, a toy that had not been gathered up by a frantic parent, an overturned makeshift stove, a partially burnt mattress.

The black and white ash that floated about settled on his clothes, in his hair and bits of grit found their way into his eyes. But it was the smell he remembered more than anything: he'd had to cover his nose so as not to breathe in toxic fumes that lingered: they stuck in his throat and made him cough.

None of the refugees were willing to speak: they were

all too tired and afraid at what would happen next. They kept their heads bowed. They avoided all eye contact.

It was the sight of the lone figure sitting on an upturned wooden crate at some distance from the gates of the camp, leaning against a wall covered in graffiti that grabbed his attention.

He wandered over to investigate.

As he approached he saw the figure was that of a boy – a teenager; he tried to work out his age, but it was difficult to tell – possibly eighteen, perhaps nineteen years; he was wearing a pair of worn out jeans and some trainers covered in mud. He was drawing: his fingers seeming to glide effortlessly across the paper.

He stopped as Tony came nearer and his eyes narrowed.

Tony noted the strong but thin, unshaven face and a wide mouth that did not smile as he approached.

'Hi!' Tony held out his hand. '*Bonjour*. You okay?'

The youth ignored the extended hand, holding onto his drawing and the stub of pencil.

'What happened here?' He waved an arm towards the camp. 'Any idea? Must have been pretty scary. Did you get hurt?'

There was no reply. Perhaps he didn't understand English. 'Are you planning on going over there?' Tony spoke slowly, waving a hand in the direction of the white cliffs on the opposite side of *La Manche*. Perhaps he could needle the boy into speaking.

That was when he'd glanced down to look at the drawing. He'd been immediately taken aback: even without close examination he could tell the drawing was good.

'Hey! Nice work,' he'd purred. He pointed to what appeared to be other drawings sticking out of the boy's rucksack. 'Do you have any more? What about those? Can I see them?'

He noted the look of distrust on the boy's face but still he reached down and pulled out one of the drawings.

He whistled softly. 'Wow! She's beautiful! Who is she? Sister? Friend?'

A strong hand shot out and Tony glimpsed a hidden anger.

'Leave that.' Firm fingers grasped Tony's wrist.

Tony gasped. 'Okay. I get it. Sorry. I was just admiring…'

The boy pushed the drawing firmly back into his rucksack.

The two remained silent for a moment.

'I'm Tony, by the way. What's your name?'

The reply was sullen, 'Suleiman.'

Tony realised there would be no invitation to friendship here.

'God! It's freezing!' He flapped his arms about, stamping his feet to keep warm. 'Where's your family? Your parents? They here?'

'Why do you want to know?' Suleiman replied with his own question.

Tony's recollections were a little hazy as to what had happened after that. He'd decided to stay overnight and spent most of the night wondering how he could get his hands on one of those drawings. With just one of them in his pocket, he knew that he'd be able to spin some emotional story that would grab the headlines.

Next morning he went to a local shop and bought some cheap paints and a couple of brushes then he went in search of Suleiman.

He found the boy in practically the same place, but he was walking away, his rucksack on his back.

'Hey! Suleiman! It's me, Tony! Remember? Yesterday?'

The boy stopped and stared, then he started to move away again, muttering under his breath.

'Wait, just wait a moment. Can we sit for a minute?'

In silence the boy stopped, then went and sat back down on the upturned crate.

Tony sat beside him.

Look.' Tony opened up a plastic carrier bag. He dipped his hand inside and carefully placed the tubes of paint and brushes on the crate, next to Suleiman.

Then he watched.

Tony saw Suleiman look at the paints and the brushes: he saw the want in his eyes.

'They're for you. Take them. Use them. That picture you were drawing yesterday – it was all about the fire, wasn't it? It must have been terrifying. Those people running away, were they friends of yours?'

Still silent, Suleiman's hand reached out and touched the tubes of paint, then he caressed the tips of the brushes.

'Tell you what, Suleiman, why don't you use these paints now, to make that picture even more dramatic.'

Suleiman's grey eyes had stared questioningly into Tony's watery blue ones.

'Finish it. Then, if you like, I could try and sell it for you.'

'How much?' Finally, the boy spoke!

Tony laughed. 'Why don't you finish it first, then we can talk. What've you got to lose?' And he grinned.

Suleiman took the drawing out of his rucksack, picked up one of the brushes. 'Water?' he asked.

'Sure!' Tony pulled out a bottle of water from his rucksack. He looked around, found an empty plastic cup lying on the ground and poured in some of the water.

Slowly and with great care, Suleiman began to use the paints.

As Tony watched, he wondered at the intensity with which the boy worked. It was as if he had forgotten where he was, the cold, the fire; even Tony's unwanted presence.

When it was finished and Suleiman had laid down the paintbrush, Tony said, 'Leave that picture with me. I'll take it back to London and try and sell it for you. We'll share the proceeds. Later. What do you say?' He reached out to take the picture.

Suleiman held on to it for a moment, and then he let it go with a half-smile.

Tony had a very clear recollection of those last few words because he had no intention of going back. He doubted he'd get much for the picture anyway, but he knew he'd get his headline story - and his much needed bonus.

Finally, as Suleiman looked directly at him, he saw something akin to pain in the grey windows that stared.

'How can I trust you?'

Tony reached into his pocket. 'Cigarette?'

The boy took one.

'Here, take the pack.'

Then, Tony had grinned and handed over a handful of euros.

'A deposit. Best if you sign the picture first, though.'

For a moment Suleiman had stared at Tony, as if not understanding.

'Here, do you want my pen? Or you could sign in paint?'

Suleiman looked past Tony into the distance, as if debating with himself. Then he seemed to reach a decision. He took up the paintbrush and signed: Suleiman bin Abadi.

'There,' he said.

When Tony got back to London, he gave the painting a title, *A Cry for Help*, and then he put it up for sale on the internet.

He'd been completely blown away by how much people had been willing to pay for it.

He'd grinned to himself as he watched the money arrive in his account: finally, he was going to become a high-flyer…

That was when he'd handed in his notice.

Next day he'd gone to visit his bookmaker.

Simon's voice broke into his thoughts.

'I remember seeing that first painting of his, *A Cry for Help*. It was up for sale. On the internet. Must have been about three years ago? I found it intensely moving. You must have seen it?'

Tony remained silent.

'Well, it was pretty amazing, I can tell you. It sold for a lot of money. Surely you remember?'

Tony uncrossed his legs. He stood up.

'Come on, Tony! Go and see what you can find out, what happened to this young man? When did he leave his homeland? And what made him…? I mean, suicide? He was so young.'

'I'd want a bonus. On top of my salary.' he said.

Simon laughed. 'Don't forget to take a hat! It can get pretty hot out there.'

Chapter 3

The intense heat engulfed Tony as soon as he emerged and started down the steps from the plane carrying his overnight bag. The glare of the sun was such he was momentarily blinded.

'Passport. Visa.'

It had been a long flight: nearly nine hours and he was tired. It was hot inside the airport: it seemed the air-conditioning unit had broken down and like all airport officials, the man was not smiling.

Everywhere, people were fanning themselves; some were sitting on the stone floor, others on the few seats provided.

Tony put his bag down on the floor, took off his linen jacket and slung it over his shoulder. Already he could feel the sweat building up.

'Reason for your travel?'

'I've to come to do a bit of research. I work for an art magazine based in London.'

'You are a journalist?'

'No. I am not a journalist. Well, not exactly.'

'Mmmm.' The man stared at him. 'So what, exactly,

are you?'

'I write articles for an art magazine called *International Horizons*. Here's my business card.' He took a card from his wallet and placed it on the desk. Beneath the card was a ten-dollar bill. Then he took out a hanky and wiped his face.

'It's warm in here.' He tried to be friendly.

The man took the card and slid the money under the counter. He looked from the visa to the passport photograph and back to Tony. He grunted and called over a colleague.

They both looked at the paperwork and then back at Tony.

Tony began to feel the perspiration trickling down his back, sticking to his shirt: it wasn't from the heat.

He tried again. 'I write articles about art. Landscapes, mainly.' His voice trailed away. He felt thirsty.

'How long are you staying?'

'Only a couple of days.'

'Where exactly are you going? Where will you be staying?'

He didn't have an answer to the last question so he took the map out of his overnight bag and pointed to the village where he was hoping to go.

'Why are you going there?'

'I'm looking for someone who used to live there. My readers – the readers of the magazine, that is – are fascinated by his work and would like to know more about him.' He tried to be brief.

'An artist?' The man's tone was hostile.

Tony winced.

Before he could answer, a soldier came towards them,

a rifle slung over his shoulder.

Tony thought they must hear his heart pounding.

The soldier came right up to the desk and touched the official on the shoulder, saying something rapidly to him in Arabic. The official looked past the soldier over to the other side of the airport where two more soldiers stood, holding guns. In front of them was a man on his knees.

Tony swallowed hard and pushed back his shoulders. He waited for the worst to happen.

The official nodded, handed Tony back his passport and papers, turned and walked away.

The soldier waved him through. It seemed they had lost interest in him.

Outside, Tony took a gulp of air. He wiped his face several times, more from relief than from the heat.

'Taxi?' A small man wearing a brown, knee-length dress and baggy trousers stood in front of a pummelled Toyota Corolla.

'Taxi?' he asked again as Tony looked around to see if anything more promising was on offer. It wasn't.

The driver was missing two front teeth, the gap emphasised by lips that seemed to be stretched in a permanent grin.

'Do you speak English?' Tony asked as he pulled out a map from his overnight bag.

'A small.' The driver held up a thumb and finger to designate a small amount.

Tony nodded and showed the taxi driver where he wanted to go.

'How much to take me there? Doesn't seem too far,' he added.

'Sure. I take you. It is not too far. You can pay in American dollars, yes?'

Tony nodded.

'Okay. That village is near the mountains. It is near to where I live but the roads can sometimes be dangerous. *Inch Allah*, it shouldn't take us too long, but in case you get killed then it is best you pay me for the return journey now, you understand?'

After they had agreed on a price, Tony gave him the advance payment and climbed into the back of the car: inside it was hot. A small, toy gorilla had been stuck onto the dashboard: its head appeared to have been broken and it dangled to one side. Hanging from the rear-view mirror was a religious car pendant.

When Tony took out his laptop, the driver shook his finger. 'It doesn't work here.'

'What, not at all?'

'Only sometimes.' The driver raised his shoulders: it was of no concern to him, and he started the car.

The road from the airport was full of craters which the driver sometimes avoided, sometimes he did not. The heat was fearsome and dust from the roads flew in through the open car windows.

Tony wanted to take out a cigarette, but his fingers were sweating and sticky.

'Don't you have air conditioning?'

The driver laughed and put his foot down on the accelerator, 'It is better to drive fast,' he said.

The sky was of an intense blue, a blue Tony had never seen before and in the far distance he could see mountain peaks covered in snow – it didn't make him feel any cooler.

They passed through some villages where the war had left its calling card: houses reduced to heaps of brown rubble, bright coloured curtains now in shreds that clung to poles still attached to broken walls, ornate wrought-iron balconies suspended in space and seeming to wave at passers-by.

He saw the sandbags still piled up outside what had once been a front door, sofas flung onto the side of the road where children were playing hide and seek and catch-ball, only sometimes they played the game with unexploded bombs - and sometimes they lost.

'Look out!' The driver shouted as he pointed to a hole in the road so big it could have swallowed several tanks. 'It's an elephant shell!' he laughed, and Tony prayed to a god he did not acknowledge that he would be out of here very soon.

After a while the driver stopped the car, got out and set down his prayer mat on the dry earth. He gave Tony a sideways grin. 'Don't worry. We are safe. The shooting has stopped. All the politicians, they are talking.'

He went to kneel before adding, 'Allah will make sure we are safe.'

Tony's shirt clung to him as the perspiration trickled down the side of his face. His bottled water was warm and he was hungry. Also, he had no faith in Allah.

When he had finished his prayer and returned to the car, the driver asked, 'Tonight, you sleep where?'

Tony sighed. He'd hoped to be able to get back to town. He was clinging to the thought of a cold shower and a bed in an air-conditioned room.

The driver shook his head. 'It's too late to go back to the town now, and anyway we arrive shortly. But you must not worry. I know a place. I will take you.'

As Tony discovered, there was to be no cold shower and no air-conditioned room.

Instead he was offered some water in which to wash his hands and face and, later, a meal of rice with vegetables and lamb.

The bed he had been hoping for was a simple mattress placed on the flat roof of the house belonging to the taxi driver's cousin.

Tony spent a sleepless night staring up at a sky of black velvet where stars jostled for space, smoking half of what was left of his pack of cigarettes, pulling hard and watching the tiny embers drift into the night sky.

Next morning, after the muezzin's dawn call to prayer spread across the valley, a veiled woman offered him a glass of hot, sweet tea with a savoury pastry filled with meat.

He thanked her and took it outside into the courtyard where the air was still cool and where some children were kicking a ball around. They stopped as soon as they saw Tony. One of the boys came towards him, followed closely by his friends.

'You, English?' the boy asked. He was grinning widely.

'Yes.' Tony replied, frowning.

The boy turned to look at his friends as they all shouted something to him in Arabic.

The boy turned back to Tony and shouted, 'Manchester United!'

With that the boys all lifted their arms into the air and cheered.

Tony smiled briefly: he had no interest in football.

Satisfied, the boys went back to their game.

The taxi driver was waiting for him outside, still grinning widely.

'Did you sleep well, my friend?'

Tony took out his wallet and pulled out some dollars. 'Here,' he said, 'will that be enough? For my dinner and... the bed.'

The man seemed taken aback. 'No, no.' he said, 'you had paid me for the taxi. That is enough.'

Tony frowned and continued to hold out the money.

The man shook his head. He put his hand on his heart, 'My cousin does not want your money.' Then he said, smiling, 'My name is Abdul.'

'Tony,' he replied, shoving the money back into his wallet. 'Don't think I'll be needing you today. I'm going to walk. I need to find someone - anyone - around here who might have heard of, or known, a boy called Suleiman bin Abadi. I don't suppose you've heard of him?'

The driver shook his head, raised his shoulders and climbed back into his car. He followed Tony at a distance, watching him wave bills the colour of envy in his thick fingers as he wandered about, wiping his face and forehead - and asking questions.

Men shook their heads and shrugged until, finally, a man nodded and said a few words which Tony could not understand.

The man pointed towards the outskirts of the village where he could just about make out the remains of a ruined house.

Abdul was immediately by his side, translating. 'This man is asking, do you mean the musician's house?'

Tony shook his head slowly. 'Musician? I don't know. Not sure…'

'He says that was the house of Yusuf Abadi, the great musician. He is gone now.'

The men exchanged some more words. 'He says he thinks that the boy you are looking for was born there, in that house, but he cannot be certain.'

Moments later Abdul's taxi had stopped outside the ruined house.

Tony got out and walked slowly towards the broken building. He walked through wrought-iron gates that had been smashed and mangled, across the courtyard where weeds grew out of crevasses and where there had once been a fountain, now reduced to a pile of rubble.

He stood for a few moments looking up at the broken windows, the crumbling walls of what had been somebody's home.

Inside he saw the ceilings that had collapsed onto floors that now resembled *pique-assiette* mosaics.

His shoes crunched over the broken glass of chandeliers that had illuminated musicians and dancers.

Climbing one of the partially collapsed staircases, Tony stood at a broken window, staring down at the decimated gardens, at the pools sucked dry, at the trees robbed of their fruit.

He turned to Abdul who had followed him, and who stood no longer grinning but open-mouthed, viewing the destruction.

'Did you know the family who lived here?' he asked.

'I have never been here,' the man whispered. 'I think

we should not be here. Bad things have happened. We should go.' His voice was shaking.

Once back in the village, where every movement caused him to break out in a sweat, Tony ordered a glass of mint tea, wished it were a glass of ice-cold beer, and went to sit in the shade of an olive tree.

He cursed himself for not bringing a hat; his fair hair stuck to his forehead and offered him no protection from the sun.

'Please, may I join you?' A tall, thin man dressed in a long, flowing garment gestured to the wide stone seat.

Tony shrugged.

'I have noticed you wandering about here. You have been asking questions. Perhaps I can help?' The man's eyes were dark and shrewd.

Tony reached into his pocket and automatically pulled out a few green notes which he held out. 'I'm looking for information on a boy called Suleiman bin Abadi. Have you ever heard of him?'

The man's eyes went from the dollar bills to Tony's face and back. He sighed. 'American?' he asked.

Tony wasn't sure if he was referring to the money or to him. 'Dollar bills and I'm English.'

'You are all the same.' The man shook his head then he held out his hand. 'My name is Hassan and I don't want your money. Why do you want to know about this boy? So many have left, gone missing, what difference does one more lost boy make to you? People don't like that you are asking questions. Who are you?'

Tony took the hand that was offered: it felt dry compared to his own moist fingers. 'The name's Tony. I work for an art magazine called *International Horizons*. Here's my card.' He held out another one of his cards, one of the edges was bent. 'I'm based in London and I'm just after a bit of information, that's all. The boy was an artist. Did you know him?'

'I suggest you try the village over in the next valley. That was where the boy was brought up. And no, I did not know he was an artist. But I am pleased – for him.' The man did not take the card. He said, 'Did you know his name means peace?'

'Not sure what you mean.'

'Suleiman, the boy's name, it means peace.'

Tony frowned: another piece of useless information. 'Okay. But he was from here. I'm sure of it. I've just been to what's left of the house where, apparently, he was born....'

'Believe what you want. He may have been born here but he was brought up over there.' Hassan waved his arm, pointing in the direction of the valley. 'He never lived here, in this village.'

Tony rolled his eyes as he took a now grey handkerchief out of his pocket to wipe his forehead and the nape of his thick neck. 'Well, the boy's dead anyway.'

Hassan said, 'Many of them are dead. It happens...'

'It was suicide. Killed himself. I'm trying to find out why. Any ideas?'

'I told you, I did not know this Suleiman. Perhaps life proved too difficult for him; perhaps he felt he could not go on. You should let him lie in peace. One should not disturb the dead. Anyway, it is not safe for you to travel here on your own. Did nobody tell you?'

Tony gave a wan smile. 'I wasn't planning on staying.'

'I was a teacher here once. If you wish, I can tell you what I know. I heard things. But you should remember these are whispers, gossip, there is no proof, and it all happened a long time ago.'

'I'm listening.'

'The boy, Suleiman, he was born in that big house you saw. His father was a very wealthy man, but he gave the child away as soon as he was born.'

Tony raised his eyebrows. 'Why?'

'He handed the child over to an imam who gave the baby to a childless couple living in the next village. I've heard say that they did not even take time to bathe the child: he was handed over as a bloodied bundle. I believe a lot of money was involved. But all of this is tittle-tattle and it may not be true. Still…'

'But why? Sounds harsh. What about his mother? What did she do?'

'You are a journalist. You should know how shame can make people do strange things. I am only telling you what I heard.'

'So, that's it? The boy was born here, grew up over there and then what, he ran away?'

'Isn't it enough?'

Tony gave up, it was the heat: he couldn't think straight. He hated the relentless stream of sweat that poured down his face, his neck, his back, his feet; he hated the fact that there was hardly any internet connection; he hated the way his fingers stuck to the keys of his laptop. He hated the way people stared at him and he knew some spat at him behind his back.

As Hassan stood up and began to walk away, Tony lit another cigarette. He pulled hard, shutting his eyes.

He made up his mind: he was going home.

There was no amazing story to discover, just some unfortunate kid who'd run away like countless others to find a better life, ending up in that godforsaken camp in northern France where he, Tony, had met him.

Next morning, after another sleepless and uncomfortable night on the roof of the house, he walked back to the village square to check one more time if there was anything more he could find out before climbing back into the heat of the decrepit Toyota and returning to the airport.

'My friend!' Hassan exclaimed. *'As-salaam alaikum.'*

'Hi.'

'You are leaving us already?'

'Why? You got something new for me?'

'Perhaps,' he said.

Tony's eyes flickered with a modicum of interest.

'Let us sit again.'

Tony allowed Hassan to guide him over to the same, wide seat in the shade of the olive tree.

An ancient man was sitting at the other end of the seat, gnarled fingers clasping a stick, his body shaking as he muttered into a grey beard.

'The man who took the baby into his home in exchange for money was a brute.' Hassan paused, tipped his head to one side. 'You see that fountain over there? You should have seen it when the water was flowing... so cool... so pleasant. They keep saying they will fix it so the water will flow again, but we're still waiting.'

Tony allowed an irritable sigh to escape, but Hassan was not a man to be hurried.

'This man, this brute, he would come here to this very fountain and sit. He was mean; his wife was no better. They were hard times. You people can never understand what happened here. Who could we trust?' He paused. 'They're all dead now anyway.'

Tony wanted to go: this was no place for a decent human being.

'Perhaps you will allow me to tell you a little bit more about the owner of that house you saw yesterday; his name was Yusuf Abadi, and he was a musician. I believe he was a good man. I have heard he travelled the world, playing in all the great concert halls.'

Tony reached for his bottle of warm water.

'Yusuf Abadi was very wealthy man, and he was proud. He had a gardener called Moonif, but Moonif was a storyteller: he liked to make people laugh. His mind is gone now, but back then he would come here in the evenings and we would all sit in a circle, on this very spot.'

He tapped the earth with his foot so the dust flew up and settled on them both, like a shroud.

'We would drink sweet tea and Moonif would tell us stories of the parties held at that big house; of the music, of how the musician's daughters would dance and clap to the music. He told stories like those in *One Thousand and One Nights*. He invented much, because of course music and singing were forbidden.' Hassan stopped and shook his head. 'These things are still not allowed. But Moonif knew how to make us dream and that was all we wanted: to dream.'

Hassan glanced over at Tony as if he thought that Tony might understand. The moment was wasted.

'Unfortunately, Moonif was not careful. He spoke too loudly, and the more people laughed at his stories, the more he embellished them. But there were informers.' Hassan spat on the floor. 'May they be cursed forever. Friends tried to warn Yusuf Abadi. They told him to be careful, but he said that as Allah was his witness, he had done nothing wrong.'

Hassan sighed and shook his head. 'He was a foolish man. He believed they could not touch him. But they did; they came for him.' He stopped again and stared at the dust beneath their feet.

'They always came. They took him to prison. I knew the hangman there; he told me they'd used the strings from one of his own violins to hang him up by his wrists. There's justice for you! Perhaps Allah would have been pleased.'

Hassan stared into the distance, his eyes moist. 'His wife died several years ago, but his daughters... they came back for the daughters.'

'The daughters?'

'Two of them, murdered. The third - they say she got away.' Hassan raised his shoulders. 'Who knows?'

Suddenly, the ancient one who had been sitting at the other end of the bench stood, and for a few moments his legs wavered back and forth as he leaned on his stick before he shuffled off, muttering to himself.

Tony stood too. He'd had enough. The heat, the pointless journey. For once in his life he'd have to go back empty-handed and renounce the thought of any bonus.

He offered his hand to Hassan. 'Thanks for your help. Sure you won't take any money?'

'Goodbye my friend. May Allah keep you safe and may you have a long and beautiful life.'

Had Tony waited a little longer, Hassan might have revealed that the one who was now shuffling away had once been a gardener, and that his name was Moonif.

Chapter 4

It is often believed that babies have no recollection, that babies have no memories.

Suleiman remembered.

He remembered his parents' heads locked together over his cot as they whispered fiercely to one another:

'Why does the child not cry?'

'You, you are a woman, you should know why he does not cry.'

'We should never have accepted…'

'You were happy to take the money, as I recall.'

He remembered his father's swarthy face looming over him, his unshaven cheeks, his voice a dark whisper, 'Cry, damn you! Why won't you cry?'

He remembered how he would clench his tiny fists, holding them close to his chest watching his mother's face descend closer to his, lips peeled back.

'Cry! All babies cry! What is wrong with you? It must be evil that has entered into you. Perhaps the money was cursed? Perhaps the child is cursed? We should never have accepted.'

Because he did not understand what - or who - evil

was, he would look up at them both and smile.

When he started to walk no loving hands stood by outstretched and at the ready; no shrill voices shouted words of encouragement. So he would fall on the stony ground and look down with amazement at his chubby, grazed hands and then his wide eyes, the colour of the sky on a rainy day, would look upwards at the figure of his mother standing in the shadows, arms folded, before she turned and walked away.

Still he did not cry.

Evil stayed.

Lying in his cot as the blood red morning light spread across the full width of the sky and the muezzin's call to prayer echoed through the valley, he would watch the sun rise, rich and intense before it threw its merciless heat down onto the fields and the distant mountains.

His young life developed gradually into a daily routine: the only servant coming to take him from the cot to the kitchen where he breathed in the sweet smell of baking bread and pastries. She was a neighbour's daughter, a foolish girl with a barren heart and she was paid a pittance, but she cooked well and she cleaned; nobody loved her and, in turn, she loved nobody.

Sometimes his father would come into the kitchen where the thick stone walls kept the heat away and he would ask the girl, 'Nadia, has he cried today?' and Nadia would shake her stupid head and his father would walk over and hit him about the ears, the shoulders, the legs, anywhere his big, lumpish arms could reach.

Once, he bent down to pick the boy up so he could throw him against the wall, but Nadia shouted: she had just cleaned up and did not want any more mess.

When he reached school age, it was a marvel to him to watch the other boys laugh and play. In the beginning they welcomed him and asked him to join them, and although deep inside him he wanted to, still he hung back: what would they say if they discovered he could not cry?

Instead, he would stand and stare at them, saying nothing.

At first the other boys did not mind, then there were whispers that this new boy thought he was above them, so they began to jeer at him and call him names and throw sticks. They were always surprised that he did not cry, but he had had early lessons in survival and defence, and he put them to good use: his young fists were like hammers, small but efficient.

When one of the older boys, Ahmed, a heavyset boy with the instinct of a persecutor taunted him and approached him too closely, ready to punch, Suleiman raised his fists, hitting out with such force a scarlet fountain spouted from the boy's bulbous nose and the boy screamed with the unexpected pain.

After that, he was left alone, and time sped by in an easy rhythm.

The local imam was a compassionate man, coming to the school each day to teach the Qur'an. Suleiman found him an easy listener and he told the imam how his mother had revealed to him that, because he was cursed, Allah would not want his prayers. He asked the imam, therefore, how it could be right for him to learn the verses if he had evil inside him?

The dark eyes of the imam swept through Suleiman before he opened up his gnarled hands: *God is with you wherever you are; and He sees the things that you do.*

After that, and each time he came, he would speak to Suleiman of peace and forgiveness. And although Suleiman bowed his head in agreement before this man of God, he knew that *his* forgiveness could never be on offer.

One late afternoon, the imam came to find Suleiman sitting alone on a dusty track beneath a vast cedar tree, horizontal branches reaching out to offer shade from a heat that was sucking up water all over the country. A clipped sun rested on the horizon waiting impatiently to disappear: job done.

The imam gave Suleiman a sheet of white paper and a pencil. 'Suleiman, I want you to draw a picture for me. I want you to draw your feelings.'

Suleiman stared and put a hand over his mouth to suppress a laugh; it was the same thirteen-year-old hand he had balled into a strong fist; the fist that had been stained with another's blood.

'How can you draw your feelings?'

Smiling, the imam leant forward, legs apart beneath his gown, elbows held within wide sleeves resting on his knees. 'Think about how you are feeling now, Suleiman, and draw. Do it for me.'

The light had dimmed when Suleiman finally touched the imam's hand. 'I have finished.'

The imam studied the picture, occasionally glancing up at Suleiman and Suleiman watched him put the drawing down and, bowing his head, push large, rough fingers over his eyes.

Time cannot stand still: lazy days rolled into weeks of

sustained heat; weeks rolled into months of drought covering an arid land; children rolled into men of resentment... and school became a distant memory, as Suleiman was sent to tend the few goats left in the hills.

As he grew, so did a tiny seed of rancour planted deep into his childish mind; it will be some time before it bears fruit, but it will grow in strength.

Black stubble blossomed over a stubborn chin as he ran his tongue over a chipped front tooth: another expression of his father's love.

There was a change in the air: a threat of destruction on the move.

Occasionally, gunfire or an explosion could be heard in the distance.

No-one ever spoke of it, because if you do not speak of such things, perhaps they will go away.

Yet the fear was palpable: fear of the neighbour, of what might be said.

News was difficult to come by: radios, televisions destroyed or hidden, buried in the garden - which didn't matter anyway as electricity was not constant; music forbidden, only the sound of the call to prayer must be heard; schools closed; girls kept indoors.

There was the smell of danger everywhere, and although Suleiman saw all of this, he kept his thoughts to himself: best keep your head down and go about your business, best not to stumble. Best to pray, best to be seen praying. Best not to suspect your neighbour of betraying you for a pack of cigarettes...

Walking back from hills, the sun going down and the air cooler, he would sometimes stop in the village square to sit in the dust and watch the men huddled in groups, drinking thick cardamom-flavoured coffee or fresh mint tea, smoking and exchanging stories.

That was when he first saw the gardener: a man from another village who sometimes came later in the evening, settling himself down in the dust with the other men, tucking his ankle-length garment about his sandals as he told stories that made his audience hold their hands over their mouths to stifle the forbidden laughter that forced its way up their throats, forgetting for the moment their daily fears.

He heard the men call him Moonif, and the tales he told as he waved sun-kissed hands about his head were from another world and the hungry men would sit in silence and gasp.

Suleiman, too, sat listening as the gardener spoke of his employer, a gifted musician who had been to countries many had never heard of, who owned a house with a thousand rooms where rivers of gold ran through every room, where chandeliers reflected the beams of a pregnant moon, where wide marble stairways led to paradise, where music was played and men danced with women, where exquisite meals were served, where the perfumes of jasmine and Arabian rose lingered and reached far out into a garden that stretched beyond the vision of the eye.

And the eyes of those who listened would open wide and their tongues salivate, as they remembered the taste of vine leaves stuffed with rice and minced meat, rice steamed to perfection, pastries filled with nuts and steeped in a honey syrup.

'Could all this be true?'

Their hungry looks would turn to question one

another, as the gardener held his head back to stifle the laughter.

When Moonif stood up to leave, Suleiman saw the men applaud and beg the gardener to come back soon with more stories.

Later, a thick silence fell over them like a dark shadow and their faces bore scowls: life was unjust.

Very early one morning, as a late summer sun poked its fat face over the horizon, Suleiman awoke to the sound of men's shouts that echoed across the valley followed by a curious silence: no bird song, no bleating of goat or sheep, as if the world were suspended: waiting.

Then came the pounding of shells, the crackle of gun fire and the distant rumbling of trucks on the move.

Downstairs the house was empty, as if everyone had fled.

His eyes and ears wide open with apprehension, Suleiman made his way to the village square to find out more. He saw the local men bunched together like harvested grapes around the dried-up fountain.

Sitting himself at a short distance he watched, although he could barely hear what they were saying: they spoke in whispers, nodding or shaking their heads. Suleiman saw his father was one of the men and he felt the air hanging over them thick with prophetic fear.

In their midst was the gardener. He was sobbing. Some of the men reached out to touch him but he pulled away: it seemed nothing could console him.

'What has happened?' they asked, over and over.

Someone went and fetched the gardener some tea.

Moonif's leathery hands shook, and the tea spilt over

his clothes, so he lowered the cup onto his lap and held it tight. His face and hair were covered in a grey dust; it was hard to tell if it was the tears or sweat that had created the ugly streaks that ran down his cheeks.

Once or twice he opened his mouth to speak, but no sound came out.

Suleiman sensed someone crouching next to him: Ahmed.

'Look at them! Scared witless. Pathetic.'

'What's happened?' Mutual hostility was put aside. For now.

'Didn't you hear?' Ahmed face was alive. 'They came and took away the owner of that big house, and his kids.'

'What house?'

'The one that idiot's always banging on about, always bragging, making us feel worthless. They had it coming; they'll be dead meat by now.' He snorted. 'It'll be him next. All that crap about dancing and eating while us lot starve. Yeah... Not fair.' His upper lip curled very slightly. 'Somebody had to tell them.' He shifted his eyes across to Suleiman.

'But... Why? Tell who?'

'He was disrespectful. Get it? Can't have it.'

Suleiman shrugged shoulders that were becoming wide and strong. He did not want to know.

'The Religious Police...' Ahmed tapped his nose. 'You tell the right person, and you get rewards.' He took out a cigarette and offered it to Suleiman.

'Where'd you get that? Hide it! Smoking...it's forbidden...'

'Ha!' Ahmed sneered. 'You do listen to some things,

then! You're like all the rest, full of crap and religion. I'm getting myself a gun. I'll help.'

Suleiman stood. 'Gotta go.'

Before he could walk away Ahmed pulled his arm and whispered into his ear, 'What's the matter? You worried they'll come for your lot next?'

The Religious Police: even the most devout were filled with unease at the mention of the name, yet he had never imagined, never thought... It was right of course; he knew the Qur'an. One must have respect; everyone must have respect.

As he sat leaning against a dry-stone wall, forgetting to watch the few goats with their small black bodies and snow-white ears, the question looped around and around in his head. He thought of his father, he did not always pray, did he? What if someone found out? And what about his mother? What if someone told them: informed the Religious Police?

He lay in his bed that night and despite the heat his body shook.

Next morning, he waited until his father was dipping bread into the bowl that held the thick, dark coffee to ask, 'Father, you were there yesterday. I saw you, with all those men. And that gardener, he was crying. Do you know why? Was it because he does not pray to Allah? But you don't pray when there is the call to prayer. Do you think the Religious Police will come here, too? Will they come and take you away? Will they take away my mother? I fear for you, Father.'

The pretended innocence of it!

His father paused; a look of shock stamped across his

face as he held his bowl in mid-air. Did he glimpse in that innocent stare a realization of what might lie ahead?

Suleiman was careful not to smile, but perhaps his grey eyes betrayed him.

'How dare you! Those fools had it coming to them! But you, you are bad. And now you dare to threaten me?'

The bowl fell to the floor and broke and the dark coffee splashed against the stone walls. A thick hand was pulled back ready to come down and punch Suleiman one last time, but Suleiman had learnt to be light-footed and he stepped out of the way.

His father lunged forward screaming, 'How dare you threaten me! I warn you, if they come here, it is you they will take away. I will make sure of it. It will be you! Everything: everything is your fault. I wish you had never entered our house. What right do you have to call me Father?'

The words were unexpected and took Suleiman by surprise. His father caught him by the throat and was pushing his face into his own, and he was once again lying in his cot and the swarthy, enraged face was looming over him.

'Get out! Get out! I want you to leave and never, ever come back. Do you hear me? Never.'

Suleiman struggled to get out of the angry grasp: this was not what he had intended. He had thought he could fight his father, stick fear into his belly for once.

'I don't understand. What do you mean? This is my home... family...'

'This not your home and we have never been your family. Your mother was a whore. D'you hear me? A whore! No, not her.' Suleiman had turned his eyes wide with shock towards the door where there was a shadow hiding. '*She* is not your mother. The imam brought you here. We were paid! We were given money. A lot of money. We were poor and childless. In return for the money, we were told to keep our mouths shut. We thought luck was finally with us, but it didn't take us long to realise: you were cursed. Your mother, the whore, had betrayed your own father and fornicated with another man and so you were born with a curse: you could not cry.'

The man he had always called Father put a hand against the wall to steady himself. He was shaking. 'We wanted to love you. I swear to that: we had wanted a child for so long. But you… no, not you. Do you know what it's like to live with a curse? I tried to make you cry, God knows I tried. It didn't work. We wanted to give you back; give the money back but we had sworn, sworn to keep you and to say nothing.'

Silence hovered between them like a thick fog, but only for a brief moment: the man had not finished, his anger was buried too deep within.

'Your mother, the whore, she should have been stoned. Stoned! D'you hear? And her husband, your father, he was an arrogant fool! He kept the whore. So you see, Suleiman, your threats mean nothing to me. *You* mean nothing to me. Nothing.' He sneered. 'You are the cursed fruit of a common whore.'

Suleiman's feet wanted to run but he could not get them to move. 'You're lying! You're lying! You're lying!' His screams were beyond his control.

'It was the imam brought you here, with the money. Now that's all gone, there's nothing left. So push off. Get out… Out! Out! You son of a whore.'

His father who was no longer his father continued to scream long after Suleiman had pushed into a rucksack as many of his belongings as he could and left.

'I take refuge with the Lord of the Daybreak from the evil of what He has created…'

He walked most of the night in search of the imam until exhaustion forced him to stop. Finally he slept, his head resting on his rucksack. He thought of the gentle lilt of the imam's voice reciting verses from the Qur'an as the sun rose with its tireless regularity and the call to prayer was heard travelling across the valley, and although his lips moved silently, Suleiman was not praying.

"*You are the cursed fruit of a common whore.*" Like blowflies, the words were seeking a window to escape.

He made his way slowly across the valley and up into the hills, sometimes stopping to beg milk and bread from a lone shepherd or from a farmer who mourned the loss of his crops: years of drought carried a heavy toll.

Several days passed. For some, those days were uneventful. For others…

From a hilltop, shading his eyes from the harsh sunlight, he could see the grey smoke below, spreading itself across the fields and villages as black objects scrambled away in haste: people on the run.

He could hear the tac-a-tac-tac of guns and he felt a tightening in his stomach because he saw the terror advancing and he didn't know what to do.

He sat against a tree, leaning on the bag that was now his home, and he did the only thing he knew would stop his thoughts: taking out some paper and a pencil, he started to draw.

At his feet was a stray dog: the animal had been following Suleiman, perhaps believing the human had scraps in his pocket which he might share. Not today; today the human held his pencil, intent only on drawing the dog, noting the thin body, the flea-bitten legs, the torn ears, the tongue that hung out. When the stone hit the dog and the dog howled with surprise, leapt up and ran off raising dust in its wake, he looked up angrily.

'Hey! What d'you think you're doing?'

Ahmed again. They are linked by a once bloodied nose.

The figure laughed as he approached. 'My friend!'

You are not my friend.

'Cursed animal! Next time I'll kill it. Ever eaten dog meat?'

'It wasn't doing any harm. Why would I eat dog?'

'Trust me, if you're hungry enough…'

He did not trust Ahmed.

'Anyway, what you doing here?'

Suleiman showed his rucksack. 'I'm out of here. Moving on.'

'Leaving? Man! Didn't think you had it in you! Why? Where you going?'

Suleiman shook his head: how to explain? It is hard to leave your home, even if it holds dark memories, and the memories he held now were even darker.

'Can't stay.'

'Come with me, back down to that village,' Ahmed was pointing to one of the distant clouds of smoke on the other side of the valley. 'See if they've been back for that stupid old man.' There was a spark of cruelty in the face hidden beneath the beard and the hair that covered a thin upper lip. 'It's seems a bit quieter there now.'

Suleiman stared at Ahmed. 'Shouldn't we wait 'til dark?'

The slap he received on the back forced him forward. 'My friend, you are learning! That is an excellent idea.'

Suleiman found they had no need of his torch to guide them over the hills: the night sky lit by an orange moon surrounded by the glimmering of a million planets.

Parched leaves from dying trees and plants crackled underfoot.

Finally, as the outline of a ruined house came into view, they stood for a few moments listening to the silence, jerking around as something shot out from the undergrowth, short legs, long, pointed wings flapping: a nightjar seeking to escape the intruders.

They continued forward, each turning his head this way and that until they reached tall, wrought iron gates that had been built to guard the house, but now stood mangled and twisted, forced open by some invading army.

Following tread-marks made by heavy vehicles, they came to a wide courtyard. At its centre a fountain, from which cool water had once cascaded from an urn carried in the arms of a naked Apollo, now decapitated and lying upon a grave of brown leaves.

The vast, two-storey house, built in a time of infinite wealth surrounded the courtyard on three sides. White jasmine and scarlet roses had once climbed its walls - starved of water for so long, they now hung flowerless and unloved.

Open-mouthed, Suleiman stared up at the tall windows, seeing the designs carved into the stone: he had not known it was possible to live within such beauty.

A tall archway of brown and black marble beckoned them through a front door that stood open in welcome, although it had not welcomed its previous visitors.

Suleiman ran his tongue over a dry mouth.

Behind one of the large sofas where knives had forced their way through the silk cushions was a violin, its neck broken, strings wrenched off and taken away.

He saw paintings that hung high up and out of reach on the gold-painted walls: proud Arabs astride white stallions that stared down at the invaders.

'One day, I will paint like that'. The thought was fleeting.

They continued from room to room, shining the lights they carried onto floors once polished to shine like the sun.

A discarded shoe lay by a door and he bent down to pick it up.

'Do not touch that.'

They both spun about at the voice from the shadows. 'That is my sister's shoe.'

'Show yourself.' Ahmed's voice was harsh.

A slight figure moved nearer to them: she wore a scarf which she held over her nose and mouth. Dark eyes ringed with red flicked from one to the other. 'If you've come to steal, you're too late. They took everything; and everyone.'

'Nice place.'

Suleiman turned to Ahmed. 'Leave it out. It's okay.

Please, you can come closer.'

But the girl had already disappeared into the night, soft shoes crunching on brittle leaves.

'C'mon, we could get rich here. There must be something worth taking. Perhaps that old man wasn't lying after all.'

Chapter 5

Moonif stood in the pool of yellow moon outside his small home, looking up at the house at the top of the hill: violated now.

He was grateful for the dark, so his eyes could not see the rare fruit trees that remained, forlorn: thin layers of grit covering branches that reached out to him for help, parched leaves that hung like claws clinging to a crumbling cliff, begging him for water.

Once, the perfume of white lilies had lingered in the warm air; once jasmine had embraced the walled garden.

Now, despite the aroma of cinnamon that still wafted silently above the dry dust, and the brave little, white-flowered henna that had not yet given up hope of thrusting its way back through the hard soil - despite all of this, the beauty was destroyed.

He thought his heart would explode into one thousand pieces.

He had never meant for this to happen.

When was it that the voices of the malcontents had burst into their lives?

Who was it who had denounced them?

How long had he been standing there? Perhaps a whole day, perhaps a night, perhaps a day and a night, perhaps longer, one hand covering his mouth, traces of salt dried up on his cheeks, his heart bursting out of his chest.

And Layla who sat alone, eyes empty, her silent voice brimming with questions he could not answer.

'Where is my Baba? Where have they taken him? What has happened to my sisters?'

For the love of Allah, the Merciful, had she not seen for herself? Had she not heard the gunfire, the trucks that had screeched to a halt in front of her home, the sound of men's boots, the voices of people shouting, people running; her Baba and her sisters screaming:

'Help us! Somebody help us!'

Screams that would remain in his head until he drew his final breath.

The day when nobody had moved; when neighbours' doors had softly closed, windows locked, dogs silenced and he, Moonif, held Layla close, the perspiration that comes with fear pouring down his face as he recalled Yusuf Abadi's last words to him: 'Take care of my daughters.'

A taste of vomit rose bitter at the back of his throat. He had boasted so often of this employer he had secretly envied: this man whom he knew to be without vanity, wrapped in unspoken gentleness; a man who played the violin with love; who claimed that music was the closest any human could get to paradise. A man of peace, but a wealthy man, and so jealousy had crept with stealth through a gate left wide open by mistake.

'Hey! Old man! What happened up there?'

It was cool in the night air as he watched the two youths approach in the light of the full moon, a white dust kicked up behind them: one taller, bearded and with eyes that did not smile, torn jeans and a tee-shirt with words emblazoned across the chest that once carried a message now barely readable: 'Death to ….' The other, perhaps a little younger, slimmer, broad-shouldered, walking behind as if unsure as to why he was there.

The tee-shirt came closer. 'She your wife?' He pointed as Moonif pushed Layla behind him.

'Who are you? What are you doing here?'

The tee-shirt shone a torch onto the old man's face. 'We were going to ask you the same questions. We've seen you before, in our village. Not looking so clever now, are you?'

'Shut it, Ahmed. Show some respect.'

The younger of the two moved forward. '*As-salaam alaikum.* I apologise for my… friend.' *He is not my friend.* 'We come from another village across the valley. My name is Suleiman. We were looking at the house up there, or what's left of it.'

'*Wa-Alaikum-Salaam*. I am… I was the gardener here. My name is Moonif.' He turned his face away as he spoke and fumbled with the cord of his trousers. 'What is it like… up there?'

He turned to stare unblinking at the youth who stood in front of him. 'You have seen inside?' He asked the question, although he did not want to hear the answer.

'It looks pretty bad. Difficult to tell in the dark. Who was it lived there?'

'Yes, but did you see… is there anyone… anyone left?'

'We saw her.' Ahmed thrust his head in the direction of the silhouette outlined against the door of the small home. 'What was she doing up there?'

'Were there any... was there...?'

'Dead bodies? Not that we saw. You coming?' Ahmed turned to Suleiman.

'It wasn't my fault. I swear to Allah that I would never have harmed any of them; not a hair of their heads would I have touched.' The old man slumped to the ground, covering his eyes. 'So they are all gone. All taken. He told me, he said... he knew this was going to happen.'

'Who said?' asked Ahmed.

'Who are you? I don't know you. Why are you here?' There was unease in his voice.

'Do not speak to them. They are thieves.' The silhouette moved forward into the light of the torch; she spat out the words.

Ahmed snorted and turned away. 'Screw you. I'm going back up there.' And he was gone. And as he left it was as if something dark had been taken away.

Suleiman watched him go, then he turned to face the man and he saw tears sliding down the leather cheeks.

'I'm sorry. I'd better go after him before he gets us all into trouble.'

'Stay a moment. Please. Tell me, did someone send you?'

'Nobody sent us, *Sayyid*. We were just passing by.' He paused. He thought of saying, 'It's true that we've seen you before. Back at our village. You used to make people laugh.' He didn't because what would have been the point? Instead, he said, 'I should go.'

Moonif did not listen and in the shadows of that night

whispered words tumbled from his mouth. 'You see, he came to me, my master, my employer: Yusuf Abadi. He came to me in this very garden and he said, "I am afraid", and I laughed. How can I have done that? I laughed in his face, and I even asked him, what is there to be afraid of?'

'This does not concern me... I must go...'

But the old man had grabbed hold of his arm.

'He said, "Someone is spreading lies about me and I don't know who it is or why they are doing this." He told me, "My friend, I am right to be afraid." That is what he said to me. The great Yusuf Abadi called me his friend and I am filled with shame. He was afraid and it was all my fault, and I did nothing to help him. Nothing.'

The old man hid his face, covering it with the invisible blanket of shame. 'He asked me, "Why would anyone do this to me?"'

'Stop! Don't speak any more to this stranger.' The girl turned to Suleiman. 'Leave. Get out of here. Go and find your friend.'

Moonif shook his head. 'Please Layla, we must be careful. Perhaps... Did Yusuf Abadi send you here or perhaps his friends? Your face, it seems familiar.'

'Of course my father didn't. Look at him! We have never seen him before. You should hold your tongue, Moonif. You should have learnt your lesson.'

Perhaps he hadn't, as it seemed he could not stop.

'I never meant any harm. I swear. It all started with this garden.' The arm that was encased in a once white tunic embraced the dying land that surrounded them.

'When Yusuf Abadi told me to create a garden so beautiful that even the Allah would be jealous, I was shocked. But when I looked into his eyes I saw no blasphemy. And so that is what I did: I created a garden of paradise. You should have been here then, when Yusuf Abadi would stand up there, at the top of the hill,' he waved his arms up towards the dead house. 'He would stand and he would play his violin and the notes would hang in the air and...' He smothered a cry, 'It was so very, very beautiful. And then he came, and he praised me. He said, "Moonif, how blessed you are. Truly Allah has given you the most wonderful gift." That is what he said to me.'

Moonif lowered his voice so only Suleiman could hear.

'But there was a worm inside my head, you see. A worm eating its way through, and it whispered to me that Allah had nothing to do with it because it was I, Moonif, who had worked so hard. It was I, who had felt the sweat pour down my face, my back breaking in the heat, my hands torn and scratched. It was I, Moonif, who had risen before the sun and worked until after the sun had left.'

The prolonged *churring* of the night jar interrupted him, as the night breeze swept briefly across their faces, bringing with it some of the perfumes of long ago. He shook his head. 'You cannot understand. Nobody can understand.'

Once again, Suleiman turned to leave. He had heard enough, but the gardener called him back.

'Three days ago, Yusuf Abadi came to me, begging for my help. He said to me, "Please in the name of all that is good, promise me, when they come for me, they must not take my daughters." And I asked him, who, who will come for you? But I knew, deep down, I knew and when he said to me, "You are a good man," I didn't know what to say, because I knew it was I who had dripped poison everywhere, it was I who had said things... but they were stories, they were only meant to be stories...'

The girl, Layla, moved closer and her voice was gentler now as she interrupted. 'Please don't say any more, Moonif. My Baba knows you would never have wanted this. We were so happy here.' She covered her mouth with her scarf.

But it seemed the old man could not stop.

'He wanted his daughters to go to his brother, in England. He gave me money for their journey and papers, He told me to hide everything until... He said I had been a good and loyal servant.'

He gave a brief laugh but his eyes were wet and miserable. '*A good and loyal servant.* If I had thought it would make a difference, then with my own knife I would have cut out my tongue: I would have cut it into shreds. I am only a story-teller. I swear I never meant any harm.'

He stared down at his sandals, at the dust at his feet.

All he had ever wanted was to pour colour into the grey lives of any who would listen. He had never thought of the consequences of so much make-believe. The more his listeners had thrown back their heads with stifled laughter, the more he had let his tongue run away with him, his voice becoming louder and louder, drifting away on the warm evening air as his audience sat in a circle in the village square.

Those tales were never meant to harm.

'Two days ago, they came. They came and they took

him. And they took Layla's sisters. I wanted to hide them all here with me, but they argued: they wanted to be with their father, with their Baba. They said they wanted to save him. They would not listen to me. Layla is the youngest, she stayed with me. They said they would come back for her.'

His hands fell to his side. 'And now here you are. You must take her; take her with you. I will give you all the money and her papers. Take her to England.'

'I cannot go with them. Please, don't make me.'

'Ssshh, girl. These are young men. They are strong. They will get you to England, won't you?' He paused a moment, took a few deep breaths. He stared at Suleiman. 'This is so hard for me. Can I trust you? You remind me of someone. Is it possible we have met before?'

His words continued to run into one another: he could not stop.

Suleiman gazed at the girl from the broken house who stood tall and proud.

She had a face he would have liked to have drawn.

Chapter 6

'You'll pay us to take the girl away, right?'

Ahmed was back, his rucksack bulging and Suleiman shook his head: clearly, Ahmed had no sense of charity.

The night had been long and the early morning found them drinking mint tea with the old man; the girl, Layla, dark eyes still rimmed with red, watchful.

Moonif turned a frightened stare towards Suleiman. 'What is he saying? He is making it sound... That is not what I said. That is not what I meant.'

Ahmed raised his shoulders and grinned. 'You told my friend you'd give us money, right?'

'No, that is not quite true...'

'It's agreed then.'

'Agreed?'

'We take the girl.'

'I will only give the money to Layla if you swear to me, on the heads of your mothers that you will protect her and that you will get her to England, to her family.'

Ahmed jeered. 'That shouldn't be too difficult for you, should it, Suleiman?'

Suleiman saw how the old man's hands were trembling.

'How can I trust you? England, it seems so far away. Do you know how to get there? Yusuf Abadi said his family, they would be waiting - over there.' He waved a hand in the air in no particular direction. 'In England,' he added, as if making sure he was being clear. 'He told me this.'

He was pleading now with his hands, with his eyes.

'Please, I only want for Layla to be safe. You must make sure she is safe. But you, only you.'

He turned to Suleiman but Suleiman had pulled Ahmed away so they stood at some distance and his voice was low.

'What are we getting into here? We can't promise anything! I mean, England? Besides, our borders are closed everywhere... who knows what's out there. I just want to get away from here, from this place but... England? We'd never make it. There's no way we can promise...'

He winced as strong fingers gripped his arm and Ahmed whispered in his ear.

'That man up there, Abadi or whatever his name was, he was nothing, a nobody: all he did was play music for money! Any asshole can do that. Did you see some of the stuff up there, in that house?'

He patted the rucksack that now rested on the ground, beautiful things squirreled away out of sight from the rising sun. 'Believe me, we'll make it to England, you and me, then I'm off and you can do whatever the hell you want. Trust me, my friend.'

He slapped Suleiman on the back, his voice still a

harsh whisper. 'So, here's the plan: *he*,' his eyes swiveled to where Moonif sat, watching but not hearing, *'he* is going to give us the money so we can get to England, but we don't need the extra baggage: the girl. We take her a couple of hundred miles and then let her go. She'll find her way back here, if that's what bothers you.' He looked over to where the girl was seated, her face a blank canvas. 'She looks the type to cope with that.'

'A couple of hundred miles? Can you hear yourself? That's insane! When have we ever travelled any further than that mountain?' Suleiman pointed up to where he used to look after the goats. 'Besides, it wouldn't be right.'

'Why not? To ease your conscience, my friend,' the note of sarcasm was lost, 'we could give her a bit of money, out of your share. We'll need to keep most of it back, to buy us papers. She can make her own way. She might even make it back here, to her "home".'

'My share? It's not our money to share and we couldn't just leave her! She wouldn't stand a chance... Not if,' and he had a momentary flashback of a woman being dragged along by her hair and, briefly, he wondered what had happened to her, 'Not if they find her...'

Ahmed snorted. 'You're soft.'

'Sorry. I'm not doing this...'

'Are you that thick you don't see? This is our way out of here. In fact, it's our only way.'

'Leave the country? This is where we were born, this is...'

'Where you'll be missed?' There was no attempt to

hide the sneer. 'Give me a break! You've no reason to stay here. You don't even have a home to go back to, do you?'

Suleiman winced as the uncoloured remark hit home. It was true: there was nothing. Everything taken from him, even as he watched. He'd run back home that one last time after he left. What had he been hoping for? That his parents – who were not his parents - would open up their arms to him? Beg his forgiveness?

Too late.

Who was it who had told those long-bearded men with voices that roared as they held their guns above their heads, pulling the triggers and shooting into the virgin blue sky?

Why had they come, rounding up people, searching, beating, poking as he, Suleiman, watched from a back row seat?

Their voices like wild dogs barking that there were infidels amongst them and that everyone would pay.

He did nothing when the man he had only known as Father was taken; he felt only shame as he watched this man soil himself, screaming and begging as he was dragged away.

Then, the woman he had called Mother for so many years spotted him in the crowd that had gathered, curious and afraid, and she shrieked out to him for help in a voice he did not recognize, and he turned his face away: because where was she when he had called for help?

When they pulled off her black head scarf and grabbed her by the ends of her long, grey hair, she called his name: 'Suleiman!' and he remained still, his arms hanging limp by his sides, as inside of him a voice sobbed. 'Why couldn't you have loved me?' That was all he had ever wanted.

So he remained motionless: it was easier that way.

The old man moved towards them. 'What's happening? Why are you whispering? Were you not sent by Yusuf Abadi? Please. Tell me.'

Suleiman sighed. 'No, *Sayyid*, we were not sent by the man you mention. We've never heard of him. You have been mistaken.'

'But your friend…'

'He is not my friend. Although it's true, we are together…'

'Ayyyay! Not your friend, after all I have done for you! You are so harsh! Why don't you swear on your mother's head, like this man asks? If you think she's still got one, that is.' Ahmed paused, then, 'Cigarette?'

Suleiman clenched his teeth as Moonif looked about in alarm. 'What does he mean? And what is that? Hide it. Cigarettes are forbidden, they are against the rules. You are a fool. I cannot trust you.'

'Sure you can, old man. What're your options?'

An uneasy silence fell. They sat back down in the dust and sipped what was left of the sweet tea.

There was the sound of an explosion somewhere, and they covered their heads with their hands as they waited to be hit.

Each knew they had to come to an agreement.

'In the name of God, the Merciful, the Compassionate, what am I to do?' Moonif covered his tears.

'*Sayyid*, we're just two guys from across the valley.

We don't know how to cross our own borders let alone get to England. These are the facts.'

'You must help. I don't know what to do. I'm so afraid I cannot trust you.'

'Yeah, you can trust us.' Ahmed.

'I am not speaking to you.' Moonif spat out the words as he turned to Suleiman. 'You must tell me, tell me you can save Yusuf Abadi's daughter and I will believe you. She is all that is left. It is not her fault, she does not deserve...'

Yusuf Abadi's daughter was no longer crying, instead her face was full of outrage and her eyes glistened as they darted from one man's face to the other.

'I don't understand you, Moonif. You were my Baba's faithful servant and you promised him you would take care of me. You and you alone.' She spoke with authority: she was accustomed to being obeyed.

'How can you hand me over to these... these dogs?'

'Please child,' Moonif's voice pleaded. 'These young men, they will take you to safety. They will take you to your uncle. To England. Don't you understand?'

'How can you speak like this? What of my Baba? And my sisters? When they come back... when they come back they will look for me. I must stay here. I must be here for them.'

'When they come back?' The old man coughed, cleared his throat. 'I will tell them where you are and they will come and find you. Surely, for now, we must be content with that.'

'You have been paid to take care of me. You!' her voice was shrill, it was the fear. 'And you are willing to leave me with...' she reached across her shoulder and pulled the scarf over her mouth to hide the way her upper lip curled, 'with thieves who only want our money. No. I will not.'

'Layla, you must. I have betrayed your father once. I cannot do it again.'

'Then you must come with us. You can't leave me on my own with them. Look at them! Their clothes.... They are dirty. They are poor.' She tossed her head in their direction and Suleiman flinched. 'If I go with them, then you must come too! You must take care of me.'

Suleiman lowered his eyes as the old man tugged on his untidy beard and clenched his teeth so hard you could see his facial bones. He watched him pull the girl to one side, gnarled fingers slipping a small hessian bag about her neck.

'I am too old, Layla. The journey will be long and I would hold you back. I would not be able to protect you. It is better this way.'

Suleiman watched her face fall away like a mask as the scarf slipped; the sides of her mouth drooped.

'Take these seeds. When you reach England, plant them and a garden will grow and it will remind you of here, of your homeland. You will find peace over there, in England. There is no war and they say the people there are kind. I am sure that at least must be true.'

Another explosion and a distant sky became one vast, black, smouldering cloud: someone else had just lost a home, a loved one.

'Now, go inside.' His voice was stronger this time. 'Please, Layla. Go inside. You will find a small bag and inside that bag a red balloon. You should tie the bag around your waist, under your clothes. I have prepared everything following your father's instructions. Rolled up tightly inside the balloon are papers and money your father left for you. He thought of everything: if you should have to go by sea, the balloon will help to keep the papers dry.'

'Wait!'

Everything was moving too fast.

'What about clothes? Does she…? In case…' Suleiman's throat was dry, the words stuck together.

'There is no time to wait. Her father left me a rucksack with warm clothes for the cold months and a few photos of her mother and sisters.' Moonif could have told them that Yusuf Abadi had given him instructions and clothes for all three of his daughters but he knew the other two would have no need of these now.

'And a veil?' Ahmed grinned.

'Yes, that too.' Moonif did not mention the headscarf he had pushed to the bottom of the rucksack, a letter hidden within its folds given to him by Yusuf Abadi. On the envelope, written in careful handwriting: *'For the daughters of Yusuf Abadi.'*

"Hide this well, Moonif. It is to be read by my daughters only if the terror I hear approaching reaches us. And only for them to read once they are safe." His gentle, velvet eyes had looked deep into Moonif's.

The moan caught all three of them by surprise. 'I don't want to go. Please don't make me. Please let me stay here.'

Moonif closed his eyes for a brief moment. 'Go now. Stay strong. All of you. Go quickly, before… May Allah bless you all and keep you safe and may Allah bless this child and deliver her safely to her family in England.'

He handed the remainder of the money to Suleiman, and Ahmed stretched out his hand also: it remained empty.

Moonif turned a wretched face on Suleiman. 'I would willingly drain my own body of everything to give it all to that child, to drape her in an invisible cloak to protect her. I pray that Allah will give all three of you strength and courage.'

And Suleiman wondered what it must be like to carry such love inside of you.

'Time to go.'

Ahmed's harsh voice interrupted his thoughts, and the three of them began to walk away slowly, only two of them turning back from time to time to see the gardener watching until they could see him no more, even though he continued to watch, long after they disappeared from his line of vision.

Chapter 7

Silence. Only the sound of their footsteps on the parched soil as they moved forward: crunch, crunch.

For a long time no one spoke. Inside Suleiman there was a voice that howled; he could feel his chest tighten, he could feel his eyes trying once again to cry as the merry-go-round went faster and faster inside his head: 'I don't want to leave. I don't want to leave'.

Everything was happening too fast; he had no control: decisions were being made for him.

Who was this girl they had promised to take to England? In the name of all that was holy, how were they to get there? They had no papers, no money, only the girl had money.

And Ahmed who kept calling him *friend*: he was not his friend. He did not trust Ahmed. On the other hand, his brain reasoned, these days, who could you trust? Telling the wrong thing to the wrong person could equate to being shot, strung up or beheaded. He wanted to shout out, Why? Because this, his country, this place where he had lived since birth was falling apart, and there was nothing he could do to stop it.

The fire of hate was spreading; the crying of the women, the men, the children, hurt the ears: impotent, all of them.

He looked up at the hills once covered with olive groves and trees, now a playground for guns and he wished he could cradle in his arms those hills, smell again the cool, dry air, take out his pencil and draw the trees, the goats, the wild dogs. And he remembered the old men who used to gather in the square on warm evenings drinking strong coffee and mint tea with only the sound of insects buzzing and the voice of the storyteller.

It was Ahmed who smashed into his thoughts, punching his fist into the air.

'Yes!' Ahmed ran broken fingernails across his face, wiping his nose, wiping away beads of sweat with a sleeve as he turned his eyes on the girl: she had money. He would have taken the money there and then, but there was Suleiman - and somewhere inside of Suleiman he sensed there was anger.

Suleiman asked. 'So, how do we get to this border? Which way?'

'We improvise, my friend! Allah will provide...'

'Allah won't provide a map, a compass, papers...'

'We have our phones!'

Suleiman looked down at the battered object in Ahmed's hand, just like his own: the battery dead. 'How's that going to help? Who you planning on calling anyway? Allah?'

'My friend, you blaspheme!'

The three of them stared up at the distant snow-capped mountains; the vast plains and the valleys.

What was on the other side?

Where was the border?

Where was the sea that would take them to so-called freedom?

Suleiman cursed under his breath. He'd never wanted to leave, now it seemed it may not even be possible. He wondered if Ahmed wasn't right: perhaps their best option would be to rid themselves of the girl - take her money. But that would be breaking a promise, it could bring bad luck, and he'd had his fill of bad luck.

'What are you running from anyway? What about your family?'

Ahmed sneered. 'Family? My mother's dead and my father prays to Allah all day and all night he reads the Qur'an. Why the sudden interest?'

Suleiman shrugged. 'Just asking.'

'I'm not running from anyone, my friend. My brothers left home to join the rebels in the east, so they could get hold of guns and start killing. Satisfied?'

'How come you didn't go with them?' He wanted to add, 'The role of executioner would come to you easy enough.' He didn't.

'You being funny?'

'Just asking.'

'My friend…'

I am not your friend.

'…I have my own plans and they don't include having my body parts blown to bits.' His eyes hardened. 'I want to get out of this place, go somewhere where I can earn dollars and live the life.'

'You've been watching too many American movies.'

'Do not make fun of me.'

Had Suleiman been able to see the thoughts that pushed and jostled their way through Ahmed's mind, perhaps he would have felt some pity for the bully who was leaving a place he despised because of the hunger, the killings, the drought; leaving, too, because he did not understand his father's blind obedience to a god he held in contempt because he, Ahmed, had only one god: and that god had just put his future into his hands, and all he had to do was play it right.

Suleiman saw Ahmed turn his eye to the smaller shape that followed them; a girl whose eyes were held firmly to the ground.

They carried on walking in silence for what seemed like hours.

It was the girl who finally stopped in her tracks and sat down on a large rock. 'I'm hungry.'

Ahmed pulled a face. 'We should keep going while there's light.'

'I'm tired.'

'We could leave you here.'

Layla scowled. 'I have the money.'

Was it then that the two boys realised the girl had not spoken to them since they left?

Was it then that Suleiman saw that her eyes were the colour of warm amber when the sunlight caught at them? He sank down beside her, glad for a reason to stop.

Ahmed threw down his rucksack. 'Okay. If that's what you want. Let's all bow to the princess, to the money holder.'

'You should be nice to me.'

Ahmed gave a half grin and Suleiman glimpsed a

wolf. 'This is me being nice, but we need to figure out how we're going to get to wherever we're going...'

'You've promised to take me to England.' Layla picked up her bag. Moonif had provided her with food and water for several days and the two watched as she took out a flatbread, broke it and put it into her mouth; the meagre amount of lamb and onions stuffed into it reached their nostrils.

With a cold smile, she handed each of them a piece.

The nights were clear and cool beneath the dark blanket above their heads, dotted with far off planets that seemed to flicker with disapproval.

The three hid in undergrowth sheltered from bursts of the night wind, rolling themselves into tight balls.

From the bottom of her bag Layla took out a warm scarf and wrapped it around her head and shoulders; an envelope remained in the bag, undisturbed.

It was at night that Suleiman heard her, and although he could not see her clench her fists and stuff them into her mouth, he knew. He had seen her touch the bag tied around her waist; he knew she was afraid. He had heard her whisper 'Baba' in the night. He knew her fear. He understood it.

Sometimes, when they stopped for a rest he would take out his pencil and draw. He drew their journey. He drew because he never wanted to forget this land, this country, the hills, the valleys, the air, the smells, the silence.

And he drew Layla: Layla walking, Layla eating, Layla sleeping.

Once, he reached out to touch the scarf that covered

her dark curls. His hand hovered a brief instant; then he took it back.

And so they continued to walk, to climb, their legs like heavy logs, their feet raw with blisters.

Layla's complaints dulled; she slipped once more into silence as her walking slowed.

They passed through empty villages: shells of houses yawning wide, bullet holes torn through broken walls and floral wallpaper.

They met endless lines of people with no notion of where they were heading, carrying mattresses and chairs on their heads; women with bulging handbags slung heavily about their necks; children clutching plastic bottles empty of water; a man in a wheel-chair being pushed by a young woman – a daughter, a wife? The line moving in silence; ownerless feet shuffling the dust.

And always in the background the sound of intruders on the move.

'Keep going,' Ahmed's voice was harsh as Suleiman bent down to help a woman to her feet. 'Don't stop.'

'Where are they all going, these people? Shouldn't we follow them?'

Where were the guides they had heard of?

The sound of shelling and sniper fire seemed nearer.

'We need to get to the sea.'

Layla seemed not to see or hear; like the others, she carried on, head down, scarf pulled tight over her head, shoulders hunched as her rucksack took on a thick mantle of grey dust, long trousers trailing in the dirt.

The first time they saw a checkpoint in the distance it raised their hopes: where there is a checkpoint there must be a border.

There were a few houses, trees and open fields. But there were too many men carrying guns; hidden snipers; explosions. There was too much danger: they could be shot or worse, taken and thrown into prison.

They took another route; forget the checkpoint, look for the sea.

'It's hard to leave.' He spoke to no-one, but she replied.

'There is no more music here. Only death.'

He said, 'Sometimes silence can seem like music, if you stop and listen.'

For a moment it seemed as if they might have something in common.

'If you had heard my Baba... if you had heard him play... he said life is nothing without music. I think I understand that now. But how could someone like you understand what music can do to your soul?'

He did not reply.

The moment passed.

Somewhere along that trail they passed the remains of a burnt-out minibus hit by mortar shell. More humans creeping by. A smell hovered and penetrated the nostrils: it was a smell they would come to recognise.

Layla refused to go near and climbed a small hillock to bypass it.

Once again they found themselves on their own, as the line of people vanished into the hills.

Evening fell before another night of eerie silence.

Sometimes, when lying in the black night while everyone slept from pure exhaustion, he would feel a surge of happiness as he gazed up at the immensity above their heads covered with a million stars that shone out like beacons, encouraging them forward. On those nights he would smile and whisper, 'Thank you,' even though he did not know why or who he was thanking.

His sketch pad was full. He started to draw on the other side of the paper. Everything had to be recorded, committed to memory. Nothing must be overlooked or forgotten.

'Why do you do that?'

'Do what?'

'Draw.' As he turned to look at her, she laughed. 'You have such long eyelashes, has anybody ever told you? You sure you're not a woman in disguise?'

He realised that this was the first time he had heard her laugh.

'I draw like you sing.'

'I don't sing.'

'You sing in your sleep.'

'No I don't.'

He smiled at her. 'I've heard you.'

'Where are you from, Suleiman? Has Ahmed always been your friend?'

'Ahmed's no friend. I knew him in school. Somehow we met up again. Fate.'

'Where did you live?'

'In a village not very far from yours, across the valley. Feels like it was another world.'

'And your mother, your father? Where are they? You've left them behind?'

'No mother. No father.'

'I'm sorry. Were they taken as well?'

He read the concern in her eyes and a slither of guilt

slid across his soul. He allowed it to steal away as hastily as it had arrived. He picked up a dead twig and crushed it between his fingers.

'My father wasn't my father and my mother wasn't my mother.'

'I don't understand.'

'The last words I heard from that man who wasn't my father was to tell me that I had the devil inside of me, and that my real mother was a whore and that I had been born cursed. I've thought about it many times. I was thrown onto a dust heap. And here I am today, leaving one dust heap in search of another...'

She reached out and touched his arm lightly. 'We are both orphans then.'

'Hey, you two, look, over there, lights. See, there's a house? People. Let's try, they may have some food.' Ahmed reached over and prodded Layla roughly. 'Pull up your veil, princess.'

'I'm not afraid.' She shrank away from him. Her eyes were sunken with fatigue. In a few days she had aged: childhood a memory. 'Where are the guides? Why can't you just get us out of here?'

They both heard the contempt in her voice.

Ahmed turned angrily. 'Why don't you just shut it?' The tension between them was a taut wire waiting to snap. Fear can do that.

'She's right. The guides, where are they?'

Then, 'Duck!'

The three of them fell to the ground in a huddle. Shelling. In front of them a cloud of black smoke engulfed the countryside, destroying the house, destroying the trees that had stood up against the outrage for so long, all resistance gone.

Boom! Boom! *Takatakatak...*

The earth shook. Fragments of the house flew over their heads.

Layla screamed and stretched out her arms as the three of them cowered in the dirt, covering their heads, ears ringing, hearts pounding.

Even when the earth stopped trembling they remained still, their limbs caught in time. Then their ears cleared a little. They heard the sound of people calling out, Ahmed barking.

'Run! Run! Screw the girl, leave her. We'll get killed.' Like the gunfire, the words came out in short bursts.

Suleiman pushed fingers through dust encrusted hair. 'Her name is Layla...'

'There is no god but God. Mohammed is the messenger of God'.

Clawing their way up over the earth that had moved, they raised their heads and saw.

'They're trying to carry away the wounded. There is no God but God and Mohammed is the messenger of God. We should help. We must help. May Allah protect us.'

Takakaka... takaka... takakaka...

They watched the people fall to the ground: it was a game of ninepins, only in this game the arms and legs became separated from their owners.

Layla screamed again. She grabbed Suleiman's arm. 'We're all going to die. We're never going to get out of here. Don't leave me. Let's go back.'

They ran from the calls for help: help was not something they could offer.

For over an hour they ran, stumbling, ducking their heads at any sound, Layla tripping and falling, Suleiman trying to carry her, but not for long: he was too tired. They carried on until their ears were cleared and they thought they had distanced themselves from the sound of gunfire.

Ahmed stopped. 'This is crazy, we haven't a clue where we're going. There must be someone, somewhere. Someone to show us the way. If we come across another checkpoint, they'll never let us through without papers…we're stuffed.'

'I've got my papers.'

Ahmed bunched a fist; his knuckles showed white. Perhaps he was going to hit her. He didn't get the chance. There was a sudden noise behind him and a figure emerged from the bushes: it was slim, only the slits of the eyes visible through a makeshift mask. The figure was pointing a gun at them.

From over their heads a bird of prey swooped down low, then rose up again to freedom.

They froze.

'Who are you? What are you doing here?'

'We're going home; taking our sister.' Suleiman placed a hand on Layla's shoulder. Was it to stop her body or his own hand from shaking?

'Home? Where's that?' The voice was highly pitched.

'Why should I tell you?'

'You must come with me.'

It was difficult to think clearly with the gun pointing

at them.

Layla pulled her veil closer.

With one hand the figure shook the gun indicating they should walk in front.

Ahmed whispered to Suleiman. 'Look at him, for God's sake: a kid with a gun. He probably doesn't even know how to use it.'

The voice behind them shrieked, 'Quiet!' A shot was fired into the air.

Layla stumbled as they were forced along a dust path that lead up towards what appeared to be a highway. Open fields came into view to their left and to their right.

Suleiman stopped and turned to face the gun. 'Who are you? Where are you taking us?'

The slim figure hesitated, dark eyes darting from Ahmed to Suleiman. 'Keep moving.'

'No.' Suleiman stopped and thought the other must hear his pounding heart. 'Where are you taking us?'

'You are forgetting I have the gun.'

'No, I'm not forgetting. Just answer the question.'

'You say you're going home?'

'That's right.'

'You are lying. There are no homes here, no homes left standing.'

'What's it to you where we're going anyway?' Ahmed spoke.

The kid swung the gun around to point it at Ahmed's chest. 'Come nearer and I will shoot.'

Ahmed raised his arms in mock horror. 'So you have a gun! We've been shot at before; we've no food and no water. So what the hell d'you think we care about a stupid kid like you?'

The child sneered and pulled off the filthy handkerchief that covered his face. 'Who you calling stupid?' He lifted his head and pointed a chin covered in a peachy fuzz at Layla. 'She's not your sister. How much do you want for her?'

'Depends how much you're offering.' Ahmed's face slipped into a half grin.

The grin was short-lived: it was Layla who moved, and suddenly the child had dropped the gun and was on the floor, groaning, and everything went quiet as if the distant hills, too, were holding their breath.

The boys stared down: there was blood.

Layla stepped back, her eyes wide with shock as the small knife slipped like silk from her fingers. She put a hand over her mouth.

Suleiman was the first to move. He bent down, listening. 'He's breathing.'

Ahmed turned angrily to Layla. 'What the…? He's already fired a shot – there'll be others. Someone will have heard; they'll come looking.'

Suleiman turned the boy over. 'I think he's okay. Think he's just fainted. Doesn't look as if the knife went in deep.'

'As God is my witness, I didn't mean…' Her voice shook.

'Where'd she get the knife anyway?'

Her voice was a whisper: 'Moonif. He said, just in case…'

Ahmed snarled. 'If you were going to use it why didn't you do a proper job? I knew we should've got rid of you…'

There was another sound. They turned. Ahmed

picked up the gun the boy had dropped. He pointed it.

'The bullets are blanks.' A large man dressed in combat gear stepped forward. 'Mine is fully loaded.' He stared at the figure lying on the ground, then looked at the three of them. 'What happened?'

The boys looked at one another.

It was Layla who cried out. 'It was an accident. I swear to you. You must believe me, *Sayyid*. Come, look. He is not dead. He came at us. He was going to shoot. He just appeared, from nowhere. Please, you must believe me.' She paused, breathless.

'This our sister. We're taking her back home.' Suleiman felt the sweat tickling down his face, his back.

The body groaned.

Suleiman thought Layla looked taller as she spoke to the man. 'Forgive me, *Sayyid*. Please, please. I was so afraid. I did not mean to hurt him. You have a doctor, perhaps?'

For a few moments the other remained silent, rough hand tugging on a bedraggled beard. 'The boy is my nephew. He is young; stupid. His name is Kamal. There are no doctors here, only people running away.' He pulled a rag from about his neck and threw it at Layla. 'Stop the bleeding and I may consider saving your life. The boy's father will want compensation but that can be settled easily. I'll take the girl in payment.'

'No!' She put a hand to her mouth.

Suleiman said quietly. 'That's not on offer.'

'Perhaps we could make a deal?' Ahmed again.

'I don't make deals. What are you doing here anyway?'

'Like I said, we're taking our sister home.' Suleiman

tried to stop the tremor in his voice.

'Do I look a fool? So, like *I* said', and the man pointed to their rucksacks. 'What are you doing here?'

'Please, *Sayyid*,' Suleiman was polite. 'Please let us go on our way. We're sorry for the boy, but he is not badly hurt. Perhaps we can give you a little money, to pay for…?'

'Seems to me you might be going on a long journey.'

'No…'

'Where's your guide?'

'Guide? We have no guide.'

'Perhaps you need one?'

'What if we did?'

The man shrugged heavy shoulders. 'Perhaps it could make a difference between your life and your death. The wild dogs out here are hungry and three dead bodies would make a good meal. Four if we count Kamal.'

'And what wild dogs would they be?'

'Let us sit.' The man squatted on the stony ground holding the rifle over his crossed legs. The boy groaned. 'Be quiet, you idiot!'

Layla remained standing.

'Let us consider your options: you don't have many.' He nodded his head. 'I'll take your money and the girl. How much have you got?'

Silence.

'Allow me please to explain: living here is very expensive. Dying is very cheap. Do you understand what I am saying? Should the boy die…'

'But *Sayyid*, he won't die. I did not kill him! It is just a small wound.' Her teeth chattered.

'Why is her face not covered? She is disrespectful. Is

she a non-believer?' He did not look at Layla as he spoke. 'Don't worry. When I take her I will put her in a cage for my men to admire. Then I will sell her.'

Suleiman's heart was pounding so hard, he thought it would break through his chest.

'Please sir, she meant no disrespect. We're just poor shepherds from another valley looking for safety. Tell us how much you want. But the girl, my sister, she stays.'

'Please, *Sayyid*. Have pity.' Her voice shook. Then she said, 'I am hungry. We are hungry. Do you have food?'

The mention of food seemed to displace a little of the tension.

'Oh! Would you like to place your order? Wait a second while I get out my pen.' The man stared at Layla and sneered, wiping away the sweat on his face with his sleeve. 'Do I look like I run a restaurant?

'Perhaps some lamb and maybe some rice with almonds and pistachios? That would be nice.' She was brave.

'Ha! Your sister is a comedian? A murderer and a comedian!'

'*Sayiid*, I am not a murderer. I have killed no one.'

'She's right.' It was Ahmed who had interrupted and was squeezing her arm so tight she gasped. 'She hasn't killed anyone. Don't think she'd have it in her,' he grinned as Layla pulled her arm away.

'Keep your woman under control!' The man leaned back, the gun still on his lap. 'You're all comedians. You want to make a fool of me? Okay, if that's what you want then I'll take Kamal and I will shoot you all in the belly and then I will leave you for the dogs.' He stood and turned to go. 'Oh, and I will take your money.'

Ahmed raised his hand. 'Hey man, stop. Wait a minute. What if... what if we could give you a little money? We don't have much, but perhaps... could you find us a guide to take us to the border?'

'Oh, so you admit you are leaving?' He licked his lips. 'If you have dollars, US dollars, it might be possible. I could find someone to take you. But...' his eyes shifted across at Layla, 'for the girl, a girl who has wounded one of our brave soldiers.' He shook his head.

Ahmed sighed. 'Just tell us how much.'

'I would have to consult with my men.'

'Any chance you could recharge our mobiles at the same time?'

He raised his shoulders. 'Perhaps. For a little extra...'

'It's a deal.' Ahmed held out his hand.

It was nightfall when the man came back. He brought back their mobiles, fully charged. 'Here, to show you we are not bad people. Kamal's wound was not deep. His father has agreed the boy will help you find the guides to take you to the boats: he is ashamed that his son was attacked by a woman, so the boy must show you what he can do.'

'What about checkpoints?'

'Checkpoints change all the time. Kamal knows which ones are in place at the moment, and he knows many of the guards; they'll turn their heads once they've been paid. You will have no trouble. The girl you call your sister, she must hide her face at all times. Take that knife from her. No more... accidents. And you must be watchful because even if the guards have been paid to turn away they sometimes forget… young girls are worth a lot of money.'

'So, how much?'

'One thousand dollars each for you two and for the girl, two thousand five hundred dollars.'

They gasped. 'Four and a half thousand dollars?'

He lifted copper-coloured hands. 'My friends, this is a very reasonable price! Kamal will give a share of this to the guide: we have a mutual understanding. Trust me, without our help you will never find the guides or where the boats are hidden. There are some who would shoot you on sight just to get their hands on your money, and the girl. It was your lucky day when you found me. I am an understanding man.'

Ahmed spoke up. 'We get to keep the gun.' It was not a question.

The man raised his shoulders and grinned. 'What use is a gun with no bullets?'

Suleiman interrupted. 'So that we're clear, Kamal takes us to the guide, the guide then takes us to the beach and hands us over to the boat man and that's it? How do we know where the boat will take us? How can we trust you?'

'This is a game, my friend; there is no trust, only money. I cannot guarantee where you will be going. It depends on the captain, you'll have to pay him.'

'Captain?'

'Escape is not a cheap option; you are buying back your lives.'

'How much more?'

The man lifted his arms to the heavens. '*Inshallah*. It depends on whether the captain thinks he'll get his boat back. Sometimes the authorities,' he heaved spittle into his mouth then spat it out onto the ground where it sat for a brief moment before being sucked into the dust. 'The authorities ask for much money to keep their eyes shut and then they forget and confiscate the boat anyway so our captain is left with nothing - no livelihood, you understand? How many more lives could he save if he had enough money to keep himself alive and those bastards off his back?'

It seemed the captain was a saviour of souls.

'Do you have the money?' The man held out a palm to Suleiman and laughed. 'Don't worry. I am an honourable man.'

Suleiman wondered briefly how honour came into it.

'Allow me to give you a word of free advice: make sure you have enough money left to buy your identity wherever you end up. And remember to switch off your mobiles at all times.' Then, 'I'll be back to collect four and half a half thousand dollars. Peace be upon you.'

In the Name of God, the Merciful, the Compassionate.

Chapter 8

They had never imagined it would be this hard, the journey.

It is not worth thinking about; it is not worth remembering, or is it?

The pencil continued to lay down memories onto sheets of paper covered with the grey dust of war.

It took three days for Kamal to find the people smugglers and hand over the fugitives. He refused to look at Layla: back at the camp the men had laughed at him and the humiliation had stung, but somebody had bandaged his wound.

Money was exchanged: Layla's money.

Now, they trailed behind a salmagundi of fellow fugitives. In front were the people smugglers, their pockets lined with freedom money as they shouted endless instructions:

'Switch off that mobile!'

'Stop moaning!'

'Shut that kid up or I'll do it for you.'

Night-times they were told to dig holes in the hillside to shelter from the cold, using bare hands, tearing with broken nails. Those who were unable to dig slept outside and, if they were lucky, they were still alive when morning came: no death came with a refund.

As the days passed, others joined the ragged bunch. The hunger for freedom and safety purchased with more money.

And all the time, 'Keep moving!'

Suleiman asked, 'Do you ever think of that old man?'

'What, that old fool?' Ahmed sneered.

'Do you ever wonder what happened to him - after we left?'

'They're probably playing football with what's left of his stupid head.' Ahmed walked away as Layla gasped, clasping her hands together.

'He seemed a good man.' Suleiman thought to reassure her.

She looked down at her worn shoes as she bit her lip. 'Moonif was kind. Sometimes he would show my sisters and me how to plant seeds.' She smiled. 'And sometimes he would pour us glasses of lemonade and tell us all the old stories of Scheherazade and Shahryar. We'd be so scared!'

Suleiman wanted to put out a reassuring hand; he didn't.

'It's all gone now. Perhaps I dreamt it all. Me and my sisters, we were so happy together. I think I must have been very spoilt.'

'You were lucky.' He looked away. 'You were lucky to have been so loved.'

'Perhaps. But, you know, there were always rumours about my family. My father said it was gossip, and he forbade me and my sisters to listen. But the servants... I heard some of them. They said my mother should have been stoned.' She shuddered. 'It was a terrible thing to say. I never understood why. I never told my father.' Her voice became hard, 'If I had told him it is *they* who would have been stoned.'

'Time to move on.' A shout from one of the guides.

'Suleiman, I am afraid.' Layla whispered.

He did not reply, but he took her hand. 'There's nothing to be afraid of.'

Walking became challenging. Their limbs ached, their legs shook, fear seeped into their blood, into their bones.

As they passed through places where there were houses, they held out their hands in a futile gesture to beg for food, but the houses were empty, everyone gone - safety sought elsewhere.

It was supposed to be easy. It wasn't.

Later, whenever Suleiman thought back to those days, he found it difficult to recall the precise moment when the incident happened. It seemed to him that all that time spent together was rolled up into one long journey, with no idea of place or estimated time of arrival.

It was Ahmed who threw himself down onto the ground, dropping his rucksack. They were all so tired.

'Hey! You! Get up! We can't stay here,' one of the guides shouted, waving his gun in the air.

Ahmed cursed as Layla's eyes slid over him. The veil that covered her face covered the way her lip curled. She had been forced to wear the veil: the guards screamed at her whenever she removed it. 'We don't want any trouble. Cover yourself.'

Somewhere to the west came the sound of dull thuds. They couldn't count how many thuds came per minute. The sound rumbled like distant thunder. Opposing forces searching for escapees: searching for *them*.

'How much further? Where are the boats?' Suleiman shouted, and a murmur of discontent rippled through the small crowd that dragged itself along with them.

'Not that far, my friend.'

So many friends…

'Keep up. It is dangerous to stop here.'

'We're tired. My friend here wants to stop.' He pointed to Ahmed who had not moved. 'An hour?'

'Believe me, it is better to be tired than dead. We will shortly be coming to a highway, it is very wide. We have to cross it.'

'It's getting dark. Can't we stop, get some rest? Cross in the morning?'

'If that's what you want, so be it. I have your money. Do what you like.' The man climbed onto a rock, the gun now slung carelessly over his shoulder. 'Whoever wants can stay with these fools. However, if you do, you will doubtless be killed by sniper fire as you try to cross the highway. If you want to stay alive then I suggest you follow me and we cross while it's dark.'

Some glanced over at Suleiman, as if undecided.

The guide decided for them. 'I remind you that I have your money. If you stay here and you survive you will need another guide so you'll have to pay again. And just so you know, that highway, it's called 'death road.' He turned and continued the walk. The sheep followed.

'Damn!' Ahmed stood and at the same time one of the straps of his rucksack broke, the bag opened and several items spilled out onto the dust.

'Damn.' he repeated as he bent down to shove everything back into the bag.

Suleiman gazed at the assortment as Layla's hissed beneath her breath, 'Thief.'

'So what? How'd you think we're going to survive if we've nothing to sell, princess?' He sneered as his hand swept up a couple of small silver bowls, a brooch that had once sparkled on the breast of a woman, a hand-woven scarf: all items easy to grab and stuff into a rucksack.

Layla saw the small, silver picture frame that had fallen onto the dirt. Ahmed stuck out a worn trainer to hold on to it.

Layla was faster.

'That is my Baba's! Where did you find it? You stole it! You stole it from our house. What else did you take? You're a thief. I shall tell…!'

It was not good to be accused of theft, even if it was becoming commonplace and he curled strong fingers about her arm. 'Keep your voice down.'

'See here!' She turned to Suleiman and pointed to the folding picture frame. On one side was the miniature painting of a young woman with long dark hair and smiling, grey eyes. Opposite was a lock of dark hair encased in the glass.

'That belonged to my Baba. It is mine. How could you do this?'

'Do what? The house'd been trashed. I picked it up… You'd left it.'

'Shut it. Let her have it.'

'You're too soft.'

Wild dogs would have bared their teeth.

'Rather soft than a thief.'

Layla wasn't listening. 'My Baba carried this with him everywhere. It is a portrait of my mother and the lock of hair belongs to a baby my mother had loved and lost. My Baba cried when he told us. He kept saying he was sorry.'

She turned to Ahmed. 'It is mine.' Her teeth were gritted.

'Finders keepers...'

She would have ripped out his eyes but he was too tall and too strong. With one hand he held her at arms' length: a puppet minus the strings.

Suleiman pulled back a clenched fist and slammed it into Ahmed's face. Ahmed yelled, let go of Layla and turned on Suleiman. The two fell about writhing, punching.

Ahmed grasped Suleiman by the throat and squeezed. Suleiman wriggled, twisting his head from side to side to rid him of the clutch then, with one thrust of his body he lifted up a knee and shoved it with all his force into the other's groin. Ahmed screamed out in shock and pain. Releasing his hold on Suleiman he rolled over, both hands clutching the hurt.

Breathless, Suleiman gasped into his ear, 'Asshole. Don't you ever lay a finger on her again. Can you hear what I'm saying to you?'

Stumbling he stood up, wavered, then bending down, he picked up the picture frame containing the portrait of a mother and the lock of hair of a lost child.

He handed it to Layla.

Chapter 9

It was a weary crowd that reached the water's edge: ragged remnants of a shipwreck before they had even taken to the sea.

The guide scanned the turquoise waters through his binoculars before disappearing back into the land behind them, his parting shot as he reached into the bag he carried with him: 'Here are some plastic bags, use them. If you have anything of value - your mobile phone - wrap it one of these. The sea can be very wet!'

Nobody smiled.

A deep blue sky stretched into immensity as gulls, white wings outstretched, mastered control of the wind and thermals, hovering motionless as they contemplated the human life below.

The heat was beginning to embrace them as the group stared at the boat they hoped would carry them to safety.

The sea was calm, reassuring, as men knelt down to pray for protection and women hugged their children closer, whispering words of love into their young ears.

Allah is good.....

As the runaways piled into the small boat, the captain,

a scruffy man with a harsh voice, ears that did not listen, eyes that did not see and a heart that had no pity, stood on the shoreline hastening them along.

'Do not panic!' He pushed life jackets into outstretched hands: life jackets undeserving of closer inspection. 'Hurry! Hurry!'

The guide had warned them: make sure you've got your money ready. Ten thousand dollars. Each.

Layla handed the money over to Suleiman even as Ahmed held out his hand, eyebrows raised, lips stretched to a cruel smile as he wished he'd pushed his hand up those trousers of hers on one of those dark nights: he would have shown her what a thief can do.

'If you get into trouble, call this number.' The captain - who will jump ashore before the small boat has even left the shoreline - distributed the number freely but nobody was listening.

First, get on board, after that, worry.

'I'm scared, Suleiman.'

'I know.' He clasped her hand: it was cold.

As the boat began its journey, Suleiman turned his face back to the land. He willed tears to stream down his cheeks but they did not obey, so he shouted as loudly as he could above the sound of the clapping water, above the noise of people's cries, above the sound of his secret fear as his eyes and his crushed heart reached out to the homeland he was leaving behind.

'As Allah is my witness, I never wanted to leave! My beautiful country. I love you.'

Every moment, every second they moved towards unknown freedom was like a splinter of his heart breaking away.

He took out his pencil and paper and he did his best to draw a final picture of the land he was leaving behind.

Chapter 10

Suleiman had never thought water could be so cold. They had left dry land several hours ago, the self-promoted captain pointing a finger in the direction he said they were to follow.

'Just keep on going,' he'd said. It's not too far.'

The blue skies and sun had vanished, as if to abandon them out of spite. Heavy, grey clouds now hung above their heads.

Several of the runaways volunteered to take control, although it seemed none had ever commandeered a boat before, and now they were out on the high seas and whichever way they looked, there was no sign of land.

They were packed so tightly Suleiman began to lose the feeling in his legs. There were six children on board. A baby started to cry, others followed suit.

When the boat began to list, leaning first to one side then more and more to the other, and when it started to take in water, nobody knew what to do. Some stood up and the boat started to rock even more. A woman lost control and screamed: to have come so far and now this....

When the rain started, Ahmed bawled at them to sit down, instructing them to scoop out the water using whatever they could find in their bags, failing that he told them to use their hands, which they did and they continued to howl as the salt water spilled into their open mouths and trickled through their fingers, refusing to be given back to the sea.

Finally, the open coffin that had left with such hope could no longer stay upright and as it capsized, they all fell into the slapping, cold water screaming for help. There was no one to hear. Women gasped and choked as they hit the water and the weight of their clothing dragged them downwards.

Suleiman caught sight of the baby, its arms floundering. Through eyes that were stinging he reached out to grab hold of chubby fingers spread wide open, but the child vanished before his own outstretched fingers could touch it. He dived below the upturned craft, searching, but already it was out of his reach, disappearing down into the deep waters.

Lungs bursting as he thrust himself back to the surface, he felt Layla grab hold of him, coughing and choking, her fingers clawing at his face, his arms, his head as they both gasped for air as the water filled their nostrils. He felt her push him back under the water as the useless life jackets dragged on their necks, pulling them down, like heavy, wet towels.

Then he lost her: she disappeared and he thrashed about in a wild panic.

It was impossible to recognise anybody amidst the sea of faces, arms, legs all fighting each other to stay afloat, trying to grab and clamber back onto the heap of rotten wood.

He glimpsed Ahmed, rucksack still over his shoulders, life jacket sucking up water as his head was pulled backwards: he heard him shout for help, saw him rip off the useless life preserver and push a fellow fugitive under as he tried to save himself, pushing the other back down using his body to clamber aboard the upturned coffin.

Then Suleiman saw Ahmed reach out to Layla and drag her up next to him.

Ahmed had lost his gun. He'd hidden it in his belt and it had fallen out; fallen when Layla had grabbed hold of him and, instead of making sure the gun was secure, he'd taken hold of her and the gun had fallen deep down into the sea and he had Layla in his arms. He had rescued her and he had seen Suleiman staring at him as the water went over his head as he struggled to keep hold of the side of the boat.

Suleiman knew he was staring into the abyss: this was the end. He would not be able to take Layla to safety; it would all have been for nothing. He tried to swim across to where he could see her, but other bodies were getting in his way. He held up a woman by putting an arm about her neck, but he was losing his strength and his legs were kicking and kicking as he tried to keep her afloat.

There was no way of knowing how long they drifted, freezing fingers clinging to the wreckage. And still the rain poured down, relentless.

Once, Layla tried to grasp Suleiman's hand and pull him out of the water, up onto the upturned coffin, but Ahmed roared that there was no more room.

That was when Suleiman understood that Ahmed would take her from him and he screamed at Ahmed, 'She is mine.'

His screams were choked with salt water and rain and he thought that Ahmed had not heard him above the cries of the others.

He was wrong.

After a while the rain slowed to a light drizzle and the only sound was that of the sea water slapping against the upturned frame and the occasional choked sob.

Life and death mingled and reached out to immortality.

It was a coast guard vessel that rescued them. Someone, somewhere had seen; someone, somewhere had heard. Their deliverers dived deep into the waters, searching for the lost ones, but the sea had claimed them for its own and in the end it was only the living they took on board.

Afterwards, someone said they could not have been drifting for very long, although it was difficult to tell as there was no sun, only the heavy, low clouds; even so, it was more than enough time in which to drown.

The women continued to wail and call out for husbands, sons, children and the men took up the same cry: why had Allah done this to them? They meant no harm, they sought only a new beginning. Was it so much to ask?

Someone cried out, 'In the name of Allah, the Most Beneficent, the Most Merciful'.

Others just stared, shivering and confused.

At the rescue centre they were handed bottles of

drinking water, foil blankets and some dry biscuits.

Layla's teeth were chattering with cold and with fear.

'Where are we? Are we safe now? What are they saying? I don't understand.'

Suleiman remained silent. He put his arm about her shoulders. There seemed to be no registration, nobody was asking for their papers or even their names; nobody took their fingerprints or asked where they were from. He found it disconcerting. Was it because nobody cared?

Layla whispered, 'Are we in England now?'

Ahmed hissed back at her, 'Of course we aren't, you idiot.'

And Suleiman told her they still had a long way to go.

Ahmed unwrapped his mobile from its plastic cocoon and tried to open a map application: it didn't work. Besides, they were too weary; their shoulders drooped and their eyes closed as tiredness gained control.

'Here, take these. There are some clothes over there if you want to take your pick.' The aid worker was smiling at them as he pushed three sleeping bags into their arms. Then he gestured at piles of donated clothes. 'Please,' he said and he nodded ferociously, 'Help yourselves, yes?'

There was a permanent noise about the place: it was the sound of uncertainty and fear. It was a sound that made Suleiman's heart beat faster.

It was unsettling to see so many crying that they wanted to go back home.

Ahmed laughed in their faces, calling them gutless fools.

When one of them stood up with clenched fists

Ahmed laughed even louder: 'Hit me, my friend!' And the runaway lowered his fists because he saw a brutality in the other's face and he understood Ahmed was no friend.

'We should tell them Layla has papers, tell them she has family in England. They might be able to help her.' Suleiman spoke as Layla grabbed his arm and he saw the panic written across her face.

'Please, no. You can't leave me. Not here. Not now.'

Suleiman raised an eyebrow and Ahmed shrugged.

'They haven't registered us.'

'Not yet.'

Layla held her hand over her nose. 'What's that smell?'

Neither of them replied.

Tents of plastic tarpaulin flapped about in the wind. The rain had stopped, the clouds had moved away and the sky was blue once more.

They were given pieces of soap and when, after their first shower, Ahmed emerged clean shaven, all traces of his beard gone, dark eyes beneath defined eyebrows, Suleiman saw how Layla stared. She laughed, even. 'You look different!' she cried and Suleiman felt a knot in his stomach because when Layla had come from the shower area wearing a pair of clean blue jeans and a bright red jumper, her hair no longer hidden but falling about her face in a mass of wet curls, his heart had skipped inside his chest but it was Ahmed who had said, 'You look beautiful,' and she had blushed.

That night, under the cover of tarpaulin, the three checked on their few belongings that had remained dry, thanks to the plastic bags.

Layla turned her rucksack upside down to empty it and as she did so a damp envelope slid out onto the floor.

Only Ahmed noticed, and he reached down to pick it up. He was about to hand it back to her, changed his mind and stuffed the envelope into his pocket.

From outside floated the sound of a male voice singing, accompanied by fingers running up and down an oud. The music started off slowly, pausing for a second or two between each note, then the fingers seemed to fly along the strings, faster and faster, the man's voice starting low, rasping as he spoke of a land of lemon groves, of waterfalls and snow-capped mountains, of birds with plumages you could never imagine, of moon dragons... of home.

They turned their heads in the direction of the music and Layla whispered, 'My Baba...'

Suleiman took her hand as Ahmed stood and walked a few paces so they could not see his face. They would have been shocked to see his mouth crumple a little, because even to Ahmed, the sound was a potent reminder of everything they had left behind...

It was Suleiman who dared ask the question they had all been thinking. He went up to the man who had first greeted them. 'What happens now? What should we do?'

The aid worker did not speak his language but he gestured to the gates of the makeshift camp. With his hand he made a sweeping movement. Suleiman frowned. The man called over to a colleague.

'You can go,' said the colleague in broken Arabic. 'We don't want you here.' And he turned his back on Suleiman.

The other lifted his shoulders, 'What can you do?' and he, too, turned his back.

Interlude

There is graffiti on the sturdy pillars of the ancient bridge that disturbs the history of the monument: stone masks look down with disdain.

For hundreds of years feet have crossed the bridge: some running, some dragging, some being dragged, and others, like today, anchored.

The bridge stretches like a great archway across the Seine, its pillars bowing down into the water, before rising up again and joining the left and right banks.

A pleasure boat glides below in the dark; coloured lanterns hang from wires that stretch around the boat swaying and illuminating the deck, glittering reflections thrown down onto the dark, silent water.

There is the sound of laughter, the clinking of glasses, a band plays.

At one end of the bridge someone is playing a violin.

And Suleiman thinks of Layla, and he wonders if the water is deep. He takes off his coat and folds it carefully.

He bends down to remove his shoes: they are expensive.

He looks at his watch: nearly ten o'clock. He hesitates then starts to undo the gold strap, changes his mind: the watch stays.

The boat disappears below the bridge, taking with it the laughter and the fleeting sound of happiness.

He climbs onto the protective wall of the bridge.

He thinks he hears the violin fall to the ground

He hears the sound of someone running and shouting, 'Stop!', and he remembers their first, and their last night together: Layla's soft mouth, Layla's body clinging to his, whispering, 'Please don't leave me. Don't let them take me away.'

And he remembers how he buried his head into her dark curls.

He hears another shout, 'Stop! My friend! Stop!'

Someone wants to save him and as he lets his body fall into the abyss, as he feels the rush of cold air take hold of him, as he enters the freezing cold waters, he feels a tear slip down his cheek.

Chapter 11

When you have walked until the soles of your shoes become the soles of your feet... When you have crossed so many borders looking for a place to hide, hoping all the time you will find someone you can trust and who will offer you a little food, some water, a place to sleep...

When you have walked through burning heat with no cover in sight, when you have crossed the waters and watched people drown, when you have finally reached the safety of those colder lands, when you have been through all of this, then it is your right to decide whether you die – or you live.

Suleiman had long forgotten the promise they had made to the gardener, Moonif; it took all of his energy and all of his willpower to keep going.

'How much further?'

'Not much.'

'No need to lie to her. We don't know. Just keep going.'

'Where is England? How much further to England?' Layla again.

Ahmed opened his mouth, but he said nothing and Suleiman shrugged.

Some fellow-runaways were friendly and eager to share advice:

'We're going to keep on going north. We've been told there are countries that will take us. They will give us a house to live in, food and a school for our children. You should do the same.'

'No! Don't go north. We've been there and they threw stones at us. They called us scum and vermin.'

'We are going back home. It will be better there now. Anything will be better than this. You should do the same.'

Laughter was in poor supply. Only Ahmed appeared to have discovered a sense of humour, Slapping Suleiman on the back, calling him *my friend,* then turning away to laugh out loud as if at some joke only he understood.

Once, beneath grey-soaked skies, Ahmed stood in the middle of a busy roundabout. Raising his arms high above his head he roared at the drivers in their passing cars, 'Look at us! You should thank us for coming. We are bringing sunshine into your dull lives!'

Some of the drivers sounded their car horns, although whether it was out of support or irritation it was impossible to tell.

Ahmed shouted and jumped up and down and Layla burst out laughing, her face suddenly alight and Suleiman screamed at him, 'Stop it! Do you want us to end up at the police station?'

It was because he could not bear to see the way

Layla's eyes had come to life. He should have noticed, rather, the way Ahmed looked at Layla.

When he questioned her, 'Why did you laugh? Are you in love with Ahmed?' she turned her face up to his and sighed.

'Because it is so good to laugh, Suleiman. Your question is stupid. Yes, sometimes Ahmed makes me laugh, but I don't trust him, and neither should you.'

Later, Layla asked Suleiman, 'Why is it nobody wants us? What is wrong with us? I'm sure my Baba did not think it would be like this. Why can't you do something?'

'You should stick with me, princess. You think you're safe with Suleiman? You're wrong. He's weak. If you stick with me, then I will make sure no one touches you. Trust me.' And above Ahmed's grin, his eyes showed a hunger.

Sometimes they walked for days in the cold and the drizzle; the rain saturating their clothes.

Once Ahmed stole a pair of aviator sunglasses and put them on, despite the fact there was no sun. They did not ask him where he had 'found' them, nor did they laugh.

Sometimes they were offered a bed in a church, somewhere to put their heads down; sometimes they were offered a hot meal and a drink or a chance to have a shower in people's homes. But Layla would go nowhere without Suleiman and anyway, they were never asked to stay for more than one night.

Keep moving… keep moving…

Suleiman found a form of peace in his drawings and when they stopped for a rest he would take them out and look through them, and he would see the ones he had done of his homeland, and he would feel a hand squeeze his heart and he wished he could cry.

'Why do you draw, Suleiman?'

'I don't know. Perhaps to forget.'

'Show me again, please. I like to see them.' He felt her small hand on his arm. 'Some of these are so beautiful, they make me want to cry. Who is she?' She pointed to the drawing of a young woman: her hands were clasped and her face was looking upwards.

'I've no idea. I saw her one day. I think she was praying. I thought an angel might look down and take pity, that he might stretch out a helping hand and pluck her up into the sky, into the heavens where she would be safe.'

'You are so funny sometimes, Suleiman.'

He wasn't laughing.

'Drawing again?' Ahmed.

Chapter 12

Suleiman never counted the number of days, months or perhaps years it took them to reach what they hoped must be their final destination.

It was springtime, and even for the three runaways there was hope of a new beginning as they stood outside the camp and stared across at the cliffs that rose out of the sea, haughty and white and strong, and only twenty-seven miles away, on the opposite shore.

Ahmed wondered aloud how they could board the ships that floated below them like so many toys, and somebody overheard and said they would be foolish to try. Ahmed smirked behind a beard that had grown stronger as if invigorated.

For a while they stood in silence. Then Layla whispered, 'I am nearly there.' And she smiled up at Suleiman as she took hold of his hand.

Three escapees with three tattered backpacks.

Suleiman used his phone to take a picture of the three of them. The picture showed them smiling and waving, for once all three of them together: their freedom purchased at a price far greater than any of them could have imagined.

Later, when Suleiman looked at that picture, and as he tried to remember those days, he saw how Ahmed was that much taller than him and he noticed how Ahmed had one arm on his, Suleiman's shoulder, and the other on Layla's: a gesture of ownership.

Despite children's laughter, the smell of camp fires and cooking, and an uncertain air of optimism, they learnt that everything at the camp happened at the pace of a snail.

The sun here wasn't warm like the sun from their homeland, this sun was cautious, ungenerous: it did not share its warmth, but it was of no consequence to the three runaways. There was no shelling here and no bombing, no fear of snipers or harsh men taking young girls to have and to hold, only long weeks that drifted into longer months until the three, now classified as refugees, became almost accustomed to life in the camp: the queuing for food, the donations left at the gates at night; the small tents that flapped about in the cold air; the children going to the makeshift school with books and pencils donated by a local population who had felt the twinge of guilt.

But at night, the wolves lurked in the shadows: a pack, sniffing and smelling out the weakest.

And Ahmed was watching: the pack needed a leader.

And Layla waited. Waited for someone to say she could cross those cold waters; waited to hear that she had approval from some administrative body somewhere to meet her family on the other side. And the waiting seemed to her interminable.

'Suleiman, you will come with me? We must tell them you are my brother, right? That we are family. You have no papers anyway – so it is possible, isn't it? Please, surely…'

When he turned his head away he heard the voice of the Layla he had first met; the authority he had thought stamped out was back.

'You cannot expect me to go alone to England. What will I do without you? Promise me…'

He half-smiled and put his hands on her shoulders. 'How can I? And anyway, trust me, your family, they would not want me.'

Even so, he promised, of course he did, and he held her hand in his and she reached up to stroke his face and smiled.

She said, 'I feel as if I have always known you.' And they held each other tight, seeking comfort in a world where all of that had vanished.

'Time for prayer!' It was Ahmed. He was sneering at them and pointing to the makeshift mosque.

How long had he been watching them?

Suleiman felt uneasy. When was it that Ahmed had found religion? He had seen how Ahmed lurked in the shadows seeming to enjoy this new life as he searched for easy pickings. 'I am The Fixer,' he would say, because these days that was what he did: whatever you wanted, Ahmed could fix it for you. Afraid of no one, he had come to like the narrow pathways, the obscurity, surrounding himself with his own circle of poison.

'Suleiman, my friend. We need to talk. After prayers.'

Suleiman shook his head. 'What's there to talk about?

We're stuck here...'

'No, my friend, you need to consider things differently. Enough of this sitting around doing nothing, waiting for something to happen. I need your help: we must have money, lots of it.' He pointed at Layla, 'As our princess here is not willing to share whatever money she has left. But no matter, I've worked out a plan.'

Layla flashed him an angry look. 'I have no money left, and you know it.'

'What sort of plan?' Suleiman's voice was weary.

'First, prayers. Is that not important to you any more, my friend?'

Together they made their way over to the makeshift mosque housed in one of the tents; dozens of muddied trainers had been left outside. They kicked off their own shoes as they entered.

'If anyone picks up my shoes by mistake, I will kill him,' Ahmed hissed in Suleiman's ear.

Later, Ahmed set out his plan. 'It is very simple. All we have to do is give to those stupid people you saw praying, what they are all praying for!'

Ahmed spread his arms wide and for a brief moment Suleiman was back in the playground with the tall, hefty boy with the cruel smile and the instinct of a persecutor, taunting him.

'I can fix things for them, give them what they want. But I need help. I need a business partner.'

'Business partner?' Suleiman winced as the other slapped him hard on the back.

'While you've been sitting on your arse feeling sorry for yourself, I've been watching,' he tapped the side nostril of his nose, 'making notes, observing. You've seen the lorries parked up, waiting to cross that small piece of water. Some of them are empty, right?'

Suleiman stared at Ahmed and neither spoke for a moment or two.

'I'm not sure I understand.'

But, of course, he did and of course Suleiman had seen the hungry, angry young men lurking in Ahmed's shadows. He had seen them queuing for food, seen them sneak out under the cover of dark, and he had understood where they were heading. He would sometimes see those same angry young men the following day and he would know that they had failed in what they had tried to do

But sometimes he saw them no more, and he would wonder if they had made it over the high barbed-wire fences onto an unsuspecting lorry, and across those icy waters.

Ahmed's mouth twisted slightly. 'Thought you needed money. I'm giving you an easy way to get some.'

'You want us to be people smugglers? You want me to help you? You want us to be like that scum? You're as bad as they are. In fact, you're worse, because you know what it's like… you've been there.' He bit his lip. 'And what if they get caught? What if *we* get caught?'

'You're such a hypocrite. It would be at their own risk. Not ours. And when it doesn't work they'll still come back to us. They'll want to try again. It's a no brainer. We charge them a fee, you find them a lorry, and they climb onboard. What could be easier? We will be helping them, my friend. Think about it, because if we don't do it, someone else will.'

Suleiman shook his head, but only slowly. 'It's not right.' Then, 'Why me?'

'Because... Maybe because I've seen how people seem to trust you, and so many of them are asking me for help. I'm a generous man, I'm offering you a partnership, a cut of my money and all you have to do is find some lorries that aren't properly locked, or perhaps have storage space underneath.'

'Storage space?'

Ahmed ignored him. 'Just find a way in, then come back to me and I'll do the rest.'

Suleiman's eyes focused on the ground beneath his feet, shifting his charity-donated trainers, hesitant.

'Look, all you've got to do is check out a few lorries, or find a driver who'll take cash for passengers.'

'Don't do it, Suli.' Layla's face blanched.

'Shut your face, princess. Listen, my friend, listen to me. If it's your conscience that's bothering you, just remember we'd be helping these people, giving them what they want most, what they pray for each and every time they go to that mosque, and if they're willing to pay us, then...that is a good thing!' Ahmed lifted his hands to the sky. 'We help them and they help us, get it? Besides, I've seen you speaking French – you've learnt fast, my friend. So, if you get stuck and there's a situation, you can talk yourself out of it.'

'You really are a piece of work.'

'Don't do it, Suleiman. You mustn't.' Layla spoke but she gasped at the words that tumbled out of his mouth unchecked.

'Fifty percent.'

The other grinned. 'Fifty percent? You don't understand me. I am helping you. And I am helping those morons. Thirty,' and Ahmed's bottom lip lifted beneath his dark beard.

'Forty or nothing.'

Ahmed flung back his head and laughed. 'My friend, you are bargaining with me? If only you knew... I have something you would dearly like to have and one day we shall bargain for it. But not now. Not today. Because you need to learn. You need to be taught a lesson. God does not like to be mocked, Suleiman.'

He laughed again and Suleiman shuddered as a sense of unease slithered over him.

When Ahmed had opened the envelope he had taken, after it slipped out of Layla's rucksack, he did not expect to find much. In fact, the only thing he hoped it might contain was money; it didn't. Instead, it contained a letter written by a father who foresaw his own death sentence. Ahmed's hand shook a little as he held the piece of paper that had suffered much during its long journey. He read the elaborate handwriting several times, trying to understand, to believe, to work out what was written. It was like a puzzle and he had all the pieces. When, finally, he understood, when finally he had put all the pieces together, a wave of happiness washed over him.

'Easy. Piece of cake.' Ahmed had told him.

Only, as it turned out, it wasn't a piece of cake - or at least, not the kind of cake Suleiman was used to. Everything had to be done under the cover of dark and he needed to be nimble, dodging the spotlights placed along the high wire fence, keeping out of sight of the guards. It was the dogs that frightened him most: great, soulless creatures that barked at shadows.

Once he had found the transporter, Ahmed would send him the escapees. 'You're their tour guide,' Ahmed would laugh.

For the most part his passengers were terrified.

'Keep quiet. No phones, no noise.' He didn't need to tell them.

He would eye up the stronger men: 'You, you look strong. You must act quickly. Help the women and children climb on board. If you don't,' he would let his voice trail away when he saw unwillingness. 'But please, silence, or it will be over.'

After, he would disappear into the blackness and later, his fist would close firmly over his forty percent.

'My friend, you are helping them.'

He began to find it easier for his eyes to slide away from the faces of the ones who failed, and who came back to beg for Ahmed's help, huddling in the shadows, their fingers running through bank notes as they checked and double-checked they had the correct amount: one more time.

He saw how Ahmed's tentacles had spread, how he enjoyed being called The Fixer.

Sometimes it was the women, holding the hands of children, who queued up to push their savings into Ahmed's outstretched hand, just as Ahmed had held out his hand to Moonif all that time ago, and Moonif had turned him away.

Suleiman wanted to scream at them to stop, tell them that it was madness, tell them... tell them... but the words never left his mouth.

It seemed that Ahmed was right: people did trust him.

They trusted him to guide them, and to put them on course to what they thought would be a better life, and they would thank him over and over.

'*Sayyid*, may God bless you for showing us the way,' and he would feel the heat of shame rise to his cheeks as he turned his face away.

He needed to believe that he wasn't like Ahmed.

He needed to believe that if he didn't help, then Ahmed would find somebody else, somebody less scrupulous.

So, he did his best to ensure the lorries were safe, to ensure the runaways weren't piled into refrigerated trucks, arriving at their destination as frozen lumps of ice: he didn't want that on his conscience.

As long as they followed his instructions... He could not be responsible for what happened once he had turned away and crept back into the shadows.

All those people wanted was a place of safety, that was all - and he understood.

One evening, Ahmed said, 'Forget the lorries. It's the boats. That's where the money is.'

It was cool sitting outside the café that bordered the seafront.

From the shore, they could hear the waves, a faint rippling sound, no more. Calm. Deceptive.

'What are you talking about?'

'I've been contacted. Got this text. The big boys, they've heard of me.' Suleiman saw the pride in Ahmed's face. 'And the money's better. It'll be easier for us to organise.'

'Who? Who texted you?'

'Told you. Major leaguers. They don't give their

names. But they know what to do. They've told me how it works: dinghies, boats. They said it's easier than using the lorries. More cost-effective.'

Suleiman felt his heart beat faster. 'More cost-effective? What are you talking about? And dinghies? Surely you remember?'

'You're soft, Suleiman. We'll explain to those losers how they can get across the water on boats. We'll tell them how easy it'll be. And safer.'

'Easy? Safer? On dinghies?'

'Dinghies, boats, whatever. Listen, my friend.' *They are still friends.* 'All those losers,' he jerked a thumb over his shoulder in the direction of the camp, 'they'll take whatever's on offer as long as they can get out. These guys supply the transport and all we've got to do is supply the customers. Get it?'

'Transport? Who are these guys who can supply this so-called transport? Where are they?'

Suleiman took another sip of the strong, black coffee and wished he had never come here; he felt angry. He wished he could be back with the old men sitting in the village square, drinking mint tea in the warm evenings, smoking, listening to stories. Not here, not at the terrace of this café where, if he stood on tiptoe, he could just about see the camp in the distance. Locals called it a blot on their landscape: they were right; a filthy hole overrun with people who had no hope, of children who wore donated clothes and played with donated toys, of young men smoking, looking at you through eyes half-closed so you could not read into their thoughts. He hated this place.

He glanced down at Ahmed's feet and a grin drew

itself across his face. It was so unexpected that he started to laugh; at first it was just a chuckle and then he could not stop himself from laughing out loud.

Ahmed frowned. 'What?'

'Hey! Where'd you get those?' He was pointing at Ahmed's shoes.

Ahmed smiled and sighed with contentment. 'Great aren't they?' He put one foot forward and twirled it around to show off the tanned leather boot with the slightly tapered toe, the elaborate yellow and blue stitching covering the calf area. Then he stood, to show off the low-angled heels. 'What d'you think?'

Suleiman shook his head.

'You could get yourself a pair.'

'Why would I want cowboy boots?'

Ahmed sat down. 'Suit yourself. But, my friend, with the money we'll be getting we'll be able to afford a lot more than cowboy boots.' He looked up and grinned. 'Might even get myself another pair.'

'You're such a jerk… Anyway it's a bad idea. Too dangerous.'

'You'll be fine.'

'Not me, it's those… people.' He forgot his sudden burst of laughter as his thoughts clouded with the memory of people drowning.

'Listen, some of our customers…'

Suleiman shook his head. Customers? Another misnomer.

Ahmed continued, 'They're getting scared. It's the sniffer dogs, they're making them nervous. May Allah come to their aid! They seem to like the idea of the boats, though. I've already told some of them you'll take them…'

'Dinghies! They're dinghies not boats, and what do you mean, I'll take them? Don't you remember? What is wrong with you?'

'There's nothing wrong with me,' Ahmed leaned forward to grasp Suleiman's arm, his grip was strong. The glass of beer he was drinking wobbled slightly but it did not tip over. 'Don't ever think there's something wrong with *me*. Yes, I remember what happened. I kept Layla alive. Do you remember that?'

Yes, Suleiman remembered. He remembered, too, how Ahmed had pushed him back into the water, even as Layla had extended her hand to help him climb up onto the upturned wreck.

Ahmed was still speaking, his tone had become more caressing. 'If we don't do this now, then someone else will and they might not be as thoughtful as you.' He smiled at Suleiman. 'Anyway, it'll be double the money: they'll have to pay three thousand euros each to get a passage on one of those boats. Think about it, my friend.'

Suleiman's shoulders slumped.

'Listen. The boats, or dinghies if you like, will be delivered somewhere along the coast, hidden in the sand dunes. My contact will text me exactly where we can find them. Where *you* can find them,' he grinned. 'It'll be at night so you'll have to be careful: keep off the main road. We'll organise a small group to start with, so we can see how it works. A dummy run. Come on, Suleiman. Just think how grateful those losers will be. That counts for something, doesn't it? If that doesn't help, think of the money. You'll be able to go to England and find your precious Layla, once she's left. I mean, if that's what you really want.' He added. 'She'll probably be leaving here soon.'

Suleiman bit his bottom lip hard. 'Don't do it,' she'd said, and when he hesitated she'd asked him, 'Why? Why are you his puppet?'

But Ahmed was right: he did need the money. False papers were expensive. He had no faith in the legal system: it took too long and besides, what if they sent him back to the place they'd all left behind? What would happen to him then? No, he couldn't go back there, not now, not after all that had happened. Still, in his head, Layla's voice wouldn't stop, 'You'll get caught. Arrested. They'll put you in prison and then I'll never see you.'

'I could do it just this once.' he said. And Ahmed slapped him on the back.

That night, while he was lying inside his small shelter listening to the noises outside, the furtive rustling of feet creeping about the camp, the whispered exchanges, the distant sound of someone playing an oud, the smells of cooking that brought him flashbacks of homeland, Suleiman became aware of someone scratching on the side of his tent, a voice whispering, '*Sayyid*, Sir, please.'

He bent down to open the flap. In the darkness he made out the figure of a woman covered in black from her shoulders to her ankles, her facial features hidden behind a veil.

Stepping outside, he peered into the dark: no one could be trusted, knives were not always readily on show, nor their holders.

'Who are you? What do you want?'

'Please, I was told to come to you.'

'You've got the wrong person. Go away. It's late.'

'The man called Ahmed says you can take us.'

'Take you?'

'I have paid him; he says you are the man who you will take us to the boats. When do we leave?'

So, Ahmed had already started on this new enterprise? Without telling him?

There was a gentle movement from beneath the woman's mud-ridden skirts as she stood in the darkness. He heard the word 'Mama'.

'What was that? You're not alone?'

'It is my son. His name is Omar.'

'I'm sorry. You've got this all wrong.'

'My son, he is a good boy. I told you, it is Ahmed who has sent me. He has taken some of the payment and he says I must give you the rest.'

He saw in her fist a wad of notes which she quickly hid back beneath her robe. He shook his head.

'You must take us.' Her tone was fierce. 'Your friend has promised. You can get us to England. You know where the boats are hidden. Please, help me.' She stopped.

'Do you realise what you are asking? How old is your son?'

'Why does his age matter? He is a brave boy.'

Still he shook his head. 'They're all brave until…'

'*Sayyid,* we have come a long way. We have suffered so much. My son is strong.'

'Can he swim?'

Her voice was unyielding. 'Why does he need to swim? You have life jackets, yes? Your boats are safe?

Ahmed said, Ahmed promised.'

'They're dinghies not boats.' He wanted to tell her as well that Ahmed's promises were fragile things that snapped in the softest of breezes. He didn't.

'He says you are his friend.'

He asked, 'What's your name?'

'My name is not important.'

'Maybe, but if I have to take you along the coast and if we get lost in the dark then what name should I call out?'

'Nadia.

'Okay, Nadia. Look, it's late. I'm tired. I'll see Ahmed tomorrow but I warn you that this isn't a good idea. It is a very bad and dangerous idea. Why are you risking your son's life?'

She lifted her veil and something stirred in his memory; something unpleasant. She raised the corners of her mouth into a forced smile. 'You do not recognise me? Of course not, why would you. It was a long time ago.' She said, 'You are the child who would not cry.'

Suleiman took a step forward to look at her more closely. 'No idea what you're talking about.' He frowned as he spoke because the recollection was not a good one.

'I have watched you here, in the camp. I recognised you because you are always drawing. Back home I remember how you would take your pencils and paper and go and draw the goats up in the mountains. Your father would get very angry.' She stopped for a moment.

Despite the cold night air he felt a rush of heat invade his body; he wanted her to stop.

She asked, 'You remember the village? How long ago is it since you left? Don't you want to know what happened to your parents? I could tell you.'

And suddenly he was being crushed by ugly flashbacks, and he felt his legs start to tremble.

He whispered, 'Those people were not my parents.'

She nodded. 'Yes, I heard that rumour too.'

He stared at her more closely, trying to make out her features. 'If what you're telling me is true, why did you never try and stop him?'

Her response was careless. 'I did, once. He wanted to throw you against the wall, to make you cry. She shrugged, 'I was young, and if I had turned his attention away from you...' She fell silent.

'For years that bastard beat me. He was like one obsessed. And you... you let it happen.' He wanted her to move away, he wanted to go back inside his tent and forget.

She said, 'They came for him and for your mother. Did you know?'

'She was not my mother.'

'They came for her all the same. I saw them. It was not a good thing to watch.'

'I know, I saw it too.'

He saw her raise her eyebrows. 'You saw, but you never came to help?'

His heart was beating faster now and he wanted to scream at her to go away, to get out.

Above them, a full moon poked a large yellow face out from behind a cloud that struggled to cover it: a spider hurriedly smothering a prey.

'There's hardly anything left in the village now. Nearly everyone has gone.'

He felt an angry hand take a hold of his stomach and

give it a twist. 'What do you want from me?'

'I've told you. I came here the same way as you did and everybody else. All I have in the world is my son, and all I want to do is get to England where we will be safe. Everyone says it, so it must be true. I have saved all my money, I have sold myself, I have stolen. I will do anything to get my son to safety.' Her mouth was contemptuous, 'I will kill for it if I have to.'

'So now you have come to me for help.' The irony did not escape him.

The child stirred again freeing himself from his mother's robes; two large eyes stared up at Suleiman. The child smiled. Innocent.

'It was a long time ago, Suleiman.'

The way she said his name jerked at his memory strings. He asked, 'Who's the father?'

'That is no business of yours. He is dead.' She took hold of the child's hand. She said, 'We are tired. I will come back tomorrow.'

'There's no point. Besides, why should I take you? What did you ever do for me?'

He remembered the pain, the bruises, how his head had hurt as the man he thought was his father grabbed hold of him and shook him, shouting: 'Cry! Why don't you cry?' His brain scrambled through the memories: the man's final words: "You are the cursed fruit of a common whore. Get out... Out! Out!"

'I will come tomorrow, and the day after tomorrow and the day after that and the day after that. You will take me to the boat and I will go to England with my son.'

He thought that perhaps she might drown in the dingy he would provide: retribution could be sweet. But what of the child? The boy was there through no fault of his. Still... he could imagine.

Next morning, Suleiman saw Ahmed waiting for him.

'I've got four more. That makes six with the woman and her kid.'

'Yeah, well thanks for sending her to me last night. What was that all about?'

The sun was almost shining; somehow everything seemed better in daylight. He could think more easily, more rationally. He would argue with Ahmed now, yet, in the end, he knew he would do it: he would take these people to that open coffin and he would give them their useless life jackets and after that, wish them safe journey. *Inshallah...*

'Anyway, I can't do it.'

'Don't be a fool.'

'With the lorries, all we've had to worry about were the police and their sniffer dogs. But dinghies...'

'Come on! Think about it! The crossing's only a few miles.'

'So now you're an expert?'

'But these boats are safe, my friend, nothing can happen and they'll all have lifejackets. If the sea gets a little rough the coastguards will pick them up, and probably take them over to England anyway. So everyone will be happy. What do you want? Do you want me to organise tea and biscuits on board? Don't be an idiot.'

Ahmed pulled hard on a cigarette and blew it straight into Suleiman's eyes. 'Don't you see? These people want to get over *there*.' His long arm pointed over to the cliffs that, in sunlight, seemed so near. He chuckled. 'And with me, they get a bargain: they get you! I'm waiting for a text. I'll be told where the boat's hidden. Then, tonight, you will take our customers to their transport. It'll be dark, so make sure you've got a torch and just be careful you don't get caught.'

'Who's going to help me get this dinghy onto the beach?'

'That's your job, my friend.'

'On my own?'

'That's what you're being paid for, remember? My contacts are big players and they won't come anywhere near; their hands must remain clean. It's business. You'll be okay - you can sweet talk yourself out of anything.' Ahmed added reassuringly, 'You'll be fine. I can give you a gun if you want?'

He did not take the gun.

There were six of them, including Nadia and her son; four men of varying ages, hoods pulled tightly over their heads.

It was a long walk from the camp and it seemed that even the tall grasses that grew in the sand dunes had ears.

He had no need to tell them to be quiet as they spoke only in whispers and to ask, 'How much further?'

There was hardly any moon and it was cold. He had a torch, to be used only in an emergency. Police with dogs patrolled all along the coastline: sometimes they left the migrants alone, preferring instead to pop into a local café for a glass of wine or a coffee. Suleiman was hoping that tonight would be one of those nights.

They walked quickly, but after only thirty minutes

Nadia's son complained that he could not walk any further. His mother took him into her arms but the child was heavy and after a while she stopped. Without saying a word one of the men took the child from her and lifted him onto his back, the boy's legs dangling on either side of his shoulders, his head bouncing on the head of his carrier. She bowed her head in thanks.

A couple of times they heard dogs barking in the distance and men shouting, but they were lucky: no one came near them.

It took nearly two hours to reach the place where the dinghy had been hidden in the dunes. The instructions Ahmed had passed onto him were precise: it would be partially buried in the sand, hidden in the tall grasses. The men freed it and Suleiman saw the outboard motor. As he stood in the dark staring at it, perhaps the men saw the panic in his eyes.

One of them said, 'Please, you must not worry. We can do this.'

Another one said, 'We've done this before.'

Suleiman wanted to ask them, how many times? He didn't.

After that, it all happened very quickly. The men, Nadia and the boy put on the life jackets. Then they all stood listening, peering into the dark. They could neither hear, nor see anything. The air was still, the only sound the waves lapping at the edge of the sand.

Then the four men picked up the dinghy and ran with it down to the shoreline.

He turned to Nadia. 'Make sure the child has his life jacket on properly.' he said, because he knew how these things worked - or didn't.

One of the men helped Nadia clamber aboard,. Two more joined her. The remaining two whispered, '*Shukran,*' to Suleiman. 'May Allah protect you,' they all said to him, and he wanted to tell them that Allah wouldn't help and that they shouldn't go, but already they were in the water and two of them were pushing the boat out onto the sea, then they jumped in and rowed silently out into the darkness.

The outboard motor burst to life with a roar that Suleiman thought could be heard up and down the coast.

And they were gone.

Nadia turned and waved to him. At least he thought she did, but he could not tell in the dark. Perhaps the child waved at him, too. Only when the moon fleetingly showed its face could he make out the small dinghy with its cargo of runaways.

Later, he thought, perhaps it wasn't Nadia he had seen because they had all been told to lie down as low as possible should the light of the moon show them up.

Still, he waved back and whispered, 'May Allah protect you also,' yet he knew that Allah was not near any of them that night.

Chapter 13

For Layla, things were moving fast. Too fast. Suleiman couldn't keep up; he needed more time to buy identity papers, but it seemed that suddenly everyone was in a hurry.

It was the politicians, something to do with showing the world how compassionate they were. Suleiman wondered, what did they care about a few hundred humans parked in a camp a few miles away, across the water?

It seemed, though, that somebody cared. Somebody managed to get Layla's entry permit organised at breakneck speed. Although they had both known that one day it would happen, still it took them by surprise.

'Good news, Layla. You're leaving. Tomorrow.' The woman from the agency came to tell her. She glanced at Layla and asked, 'I can bring you some more clothes if you like?'

Layla did not like. She asked, 'What time?'

The woman did not reply to her question. 'Your papers are in order. They'll be waiting for you, over there,' she said nodding towards the elusive white cliffs.

'You should be pleased.'

That evening Layla asked Suleiman to accompany her to the showers and to wait for her outside.

All about them was the sound of people chatting, eating, laughing; they walked past families playing music, trying to pretend they were back home. This evening there was a certain happiness.

'Wait for me,' she whispered and when she emerged from the shower a while later, he thought how beautiful she looked and he took her hand. She did not take it back but squeezed his tightly.

He pulled her away into the shadows, so they wandered off the path into the bushes, and he put his mouth on hers and kissed her deeply, and she put soft arms about his neck and before either of them became aware of what they had done she was his, entirely and completely.

After, as she gathered her clothes she started to cry and he put his arms about her, 'We are together now,' he whispered into her ear. 'I will always be with you. We'll get married and have children. And we'll have our own home and I shall take care of you. I love you.'

He whispered those last three words again and again in her ear even as, once again, he took her over and over and still she cried softly.

'It's too late, Suleiman. It's all arranged, I'm going to England, tomorrow. They have told me.'

He felt her wet tears on his face.

'Why can't you come with me? You could hide in one of those lorries? Or a boat?'

'I'll get myself papers. I'll have enough money soon. I'll come and find you. I swear. We will marry. I just need a little more time.'

A little more time: a few more souls to put their trust in Ahmed.

'But how will you find me? I don't know…I have no address yet.'

'My sweet one, I will always find you. You are the other half of my soul.'

'Papers, how will you get them? Can Ahmed help?'

'We don't need Ahmed. Don't worry. I'll sort it. Once you get to England, text me where you are and I'll come. I swear to you as Allah is my witness I will cross seas,' he grinned at her and his eyes lit up, 'I will fight dragons. I will kill all who stand in my way. I will find you and together we will breathe the same air.'

He was still smiling as he repeated, 'We will be together and I will fight dragons.'

Silently she pulled herself away from him. 'You will have to do more than fight dragons, Suleiman. Now I must go back to the showers,' she whispered.

'Please do not wash me away,' he pleaded with her. 'Leave whatever life I have left in you, so we will always be together. I will find you. I swear.'

She shook her head.

Chapter 14

He should have waited for her. He didn't. Instead, he walked quickly back to his small tent, breathing deeply and still trembling.

He gave a vicious kick at a tin can lying in the dry mud, and when it didn't go far enough, he kicked at it again.

Somewhere, in another life, he'd made a promise to an old man and now that promise was about to be fulfilled and Layla was going away.

Layla was leaving.

Leaving him.

His stomach tightened with the fear of losing her and he pushed his fingers into his eyes in case of tears: none came.

Perhaps it was a woman cooking hot food for her children who knocked over some boiling fat onto a small fire; perhaps it was someone angry with the dirt and the misery who had struck a match; perhaps it was a cigarette left burning inside one of the tents... whoever or whatever it was, a sudden wind blew through and snapped at the flame, licking at it hungrily until black smoke and orange flames spread through the camp with such momentum there was barely time to oppose it.

People ran in all directions, sweeping up children in their arms, grabbing whatever belongings they could, screaming and calling out names.

Suleiman ran back to the showers looking for Layla. She wasn't there. He called her name. Then he saw Ahmed.

'Where's Layla? Have you seen her?'

He panicked as he felt the heat of the fire near to his face.

A piece of tarpaulin fell to the ground as flames licked and spattered, and he heard Ahmed's shout above the noise.

'We've a boat load scheduled for tonight. Damn it! I didn't get all their money. I'll never find them in this mess.'

Another gust of wind blew a cloud of black smoke over them.

Suleiman's scream was trapped in his throat; he cursed Ahmed, he cursed everyone. 'Have you seen Layla?'

'Forget Layla! What about our cargo? Find them. Round them up. Tell them it's still on, but they'll have to be extra careful. Fingers crossed the police'll be too busy here to worry about boats.' Ahmed frowned. 'In fact, I could charge more…'

'You're unbelievable.' Suleiman thrust a clenched fist into Ahmed's face and watched him fall backwards. 'Screw you and your sodding money. Where's Layla? She was here. I left her here.'

He turned and ran in the opposite direction, calling her name, as the fire continued on its path.

Ahmed screamed after him, 'Find the beggars, Suleiman - else you won't get your money.' He stumbled to get up, one hand rubbing a bloodied face. 'You bastard…'

The wind carried away his screams.

Later, with first light, when the flimsy structures, the tents, the self-made shops, the so-called school, the mosque had all been cleansed by the flames, the journalists arrived at the broken gates of the camp, vulture-like, arms flapping and waving as they shouted out their questions, phones and cameras at the ready.

'What happened here? Any idea?'

'How did it start?'

'Can you spare a minute? What's the story?'

They hovered, sharp eyes darting about, searching for the headline that might change their lives.

One distanced itself from the group. With feigned nonchalance he stepped over burnt fragments made sodden by fire fighters' hoses and sidled up to where, at the gates of the camp, Suleiman was sitting alone on an upturned wooden crate.

'Cigarette?' The hack held out a half-empty pack. 'D'you mind if I sit with you a minute?'

Suleiman lifted his head, noting the other's fraudulent smile.

The man gestured at what was left of the camp behind them. 'The fire, how'd it start? Any ideas?' He put a handkerchief over his nose, perhaps unsettled by the acrid smell of burning combined with the squalor and the cold.

The wind slapped both their faces, indiscriminate icy fingers creeping beneath their clothing.

'What's your name? Where you from?' The voice changed, the language cajoling. 'It's okay mate. You can trust me.'

Mate? Trust? Suleiman winced. The man took a hold of his arm; he shoved him off as you would a blowfly.

'Sorry. You're upset. Understandable. I just wondered if you could tell me what happened here. How did it start? Was it deliberate? What d'you think?'

Suleiman struggled to breathe, he felt as if there was no air left in his lungs.

The hack came closer, his voice a low whisper. 'Listen. I can give you good money, if you can give me a story. I heard someone might have died. D'you know who? That'd make a story.'

Suleiman turned, trying to move away. One minute he'd been with Layla and the next...

He'd been angry; he hadn't waited. He should have waited.

He heard voices barking from megaphones, instructing all refugees to go to the entrance gates where they would be collected and taken to a safer place.

He watched, recognising some: tonight would have been their escape. He turned his face away so they would not see him.

'Come on! You need money, don't you? 'Course you do. Tell me what you can.' The voice persisted. 'Here.' A five euro note was floated in front of his face.

He saw the man bite his lip and look around. He sensed his irritation; he knew the man was wondering if he should move on and question somebody else. He saw that the man was not patient.

'You been here long?'

'Maybe.'

'You got family here? Brothers? Sisters? Friends?'

Suleiman had learnt a lot over the past months, or was it years? He couldn't remember.

'Layla. She's going to England.'

He could have added that he'd lost her; he could had said there was one other, who called himself a friend, but he didn't know where he was either and, besides, he wasn't a friend. Under his breath he said, 'It was a dark hole of a place anyway,' and beneath defiant grey eyes that looked up at the hack, there was a wretchedness.

'Why aren't you going with her?' The man had taken out a notebook. 'Tell me about yourself; where you from? What it's like here?'

He didn't like questions.

Layla.

He stood, picked up his rucksack and pushed past the journalist. There must be somebody he could ask, someone who could tell him where she was?

Everyone was busy. People being rounded up and thrust onto buses waiting to take them away.

He recognised one of the helpers. Seeing him approach the woman stopped what she was doing; perhaps she felt compassion because Suleiman could barely speak.

'Layla,' he stuttered, 'Where is she?'

'She's gone, love. She was lucky. We got her onto one of the first buses out of here. She didn't want to go, though. Not at first, anyway. Silly girl. Think she was looking for you.' She shook her head. 'She said something about you hadn't waited for her. Anyway, you should be pleased. She'll be safe now. Well on her way.'

He wanted to sink down into the earth, the weight was too great. Only he, Suleiman, knew that Layla could never be safe without him.

'You'd better get on one of the buses,' she said.

Suleiman shrugged. Leaving the queue of people waiting to be taken away, he walked away from the camp, and wandered further down the road.

A mobile van was selling sandwiches and the smell of hot soup reached his nostrils.

He came to a wall covered in graffiti. Sitting on an upturned wooden crate, he reached into his bag and pulled out the battered sketch pad and pencil.

He drew the fire. He drew the people scurrying off like colonies of ants, but he did not draw Layla. This time he drew Ahmed: the beard, the mean lips, teeth like pitted black olives. Where was he? Was he dead? Burnt alive? Even Ahmed didn't deserve that.

The stub of pencil flew across the paper, outlining the swarm of people, mouths open in silent screams, children holding hands, a torn scarf hanging from a bush, a shoe laying on its side.

A world with no Ahmed was no loss.

But a world without Layla...

'Fancy some soup?' The man had followed him, long brown coat clinging to jeans spattered with mud and dirt. He had stood watching as Suleiman's slim hand created a picture that almost took his breath away, because even he could see the honesty in it.

When the man brought back the polystyrene cup of

hot soup and the chunk of bread, Suleiman put down his work and wrapped dirt-encrusted fingers about the steaming cup.

'*Shukran.*'

'What's your name? I'm Tony, by the way.'

Suleiman hesitated, dipping the bread into the soup, careful not to miss a single drop. Wiping a hand over the faint outline of red juice left around his mouth, he said, 'Suleiman.'

'Okay, Suleiman. You happy for me to ask you a few questions? Don't worry, I'll pay you. That fire, any idea how it started? Was it deliberate d'you think? I heard somebody died?'

'Place needed to be burnt down. I told you, it was a black hole of a place.' He put the empty cup down onto the ground.

The man slapped his hands about his arms and legs. 'God it's cold here! How d'you cope?'

Was that another question?

'Where'd you learn to draw?'

Suleiman began jigging his legs encased in tight jeans up and down; he pulled the coat that had seen better days more firmly about his shoulders, and the book of drawings fell to the floor.

The hack bent down to pick it up but Suleiman got there first.

'You've got more pictures? Can I see them?' This time the man took out ten euros and put them on top of the book.

'Screw you! You know where you can stick your euros? Layla paid ten thousand dollars to get us here, to this hole, so you and your ten bloody euros...'

He stood up, he wanted to cry. He was taller than the other man. The discarded bank note slipped to the ground.

He didn't wait for a reply.

He turned and disappeared into a diminishing sea of lost people.

That night, Suleiman slept in one of the blue tents the charity workers were still distributing. He hid the tent in a bush away from what was left of the camp, out of sight of the police who were still rounding up stragglers.

He wanted to cry because he had lost the only person who meant anything to him. He took out his phone and stared at it. They had exchanged numbers once, but he'd never used it, never called her: he'd never needed to.

He left a message.

Right now he was cold, he was hungry, he was afraid. He was an alien in a country that had never wanted him in the first place.

And he was alone.

Next morning, Suleiman saw the hack walking up and down the road outside the gates of the camp which was now empty, save for a few journalists and photographers still hanging around.

When Tony waved to him, he did not wave back.

It was time to move on.

He began to walk away, all his possessions stowed away in his old rucksack.

He had not understood the other's tenacity.

The hack quickened his pace to catch up with him.

'Hey! Wait a minute, Suleiman. Just wait a minute.

Let me explain. I was hoping to see you. Look here.' And he opened up a plastic bag to reveal a clean drawing pad, pencils and tubes of paint and brushes of different sizes.

He said, 'I think you've got talent. Your drawings are good. I mean, I'm not saying they're perfect but... hey, with a splash of colour here and there, something to create a bit of drama. You know what I mean? That's what people want to see: drama.'

Suleiman did not reply but he stopped. He was trying not to look inside the bag. He ran a thirsty tongue over his lips. He felt like a magpie that has seen something sparkling, and he longed to have it.

'Here. Take them.' The man was pushing the bag onto him. 'They're for you. If you can paint a picture then I'll sell it for you. What do you think?'

'Layla's gone.'

'I'm sorry. Who?'

Suleiman took a deep breath. 'Layla. I told you, she's gone to England but they wouldn't let me go with her.'

'Right. Okay. Tell you what, show me that drawing you were doing yesterday...'

Suleiman's mouth twisted into a bitter smile. Why did nobody listen? He reached down into his rucksack and took out his pad. He opened it up.

'Yes, that one. Look, I'm no artist but I've learnt quite a bit over the years, and I think all that one needs is a dash of colour; it'd add to the intensity of the moment. These people, they're all running away from the fire, right? They're dead scared. Finish it. I think I could sell it for you.'

'How much?'

Suleiman would never forget the man's laughter: it

carried a whiff of dishonesty.

'Well, you haven't finished it yet and...'

'How can I trust you?' An unnecessary question.

'How can you trust anybody? Worth a try though, isn't it? What've you got to lose?'

A pair of eyes the colour of the sky on a rainy day looked at the man, because what the man was really saying to him was, what have you got to lose when you have nothing to start with?

'Tell me, would it buy me papers, so I can get to England?'

'Why not?'

When the picture was finished, when Suleiman had added tongues of flaming orange and red, when he had drawn a child running, clothed in a torn faded yellow dress, when he had added a scarf coloured in blue with silver stars clinging to a burnt tent, he had to acknowledge that it did indeed add drama.

The man put a hand into his inside jacket pocket and pulled out fifty euros. 'Sorry mate. It's all I've got on me at the moment, but if I manage to sell it...'

Suleiman stared at the money. He said nothing.

'By the way, you haven't signed it.'

'Signed it?'

'Well, if I'm going to sell it for you it'll need a signature; it could add value.' The man hesitated. 'Look, I'll do my best. Can't promise anything, mind. Times are hard for us all, but if I do manage to sell it, I'll come back. I'll always find you. Trust me. We'll split the proceeds. Fifty-fifty. Deal?'

Strange that lies have no colour.

'Still, the picture does need to be signed.'

Suleiman paused for a moment, remembering the broken house he had visited at the start of his journey, remembering the paintings hanging high up on those walls, remembering how he had first met Layla and heard of her Baba.

He took a paintbrush and with a slender hand he wrote *Suleiman bin Abadi*. He stood, looked once more at the painting before handing it over to Tony who glanced at it, nodded and walked away.

The picture went viral: the internet, Facebook: everyone wanted a piece of *that* picture. 'A Cry for Help.'

Critics admired the intensity of the work, the honesty, the undisguised sadness and everyone felt the shame as they viewed the fleeing figures, the children crying, the camp burning, the single forgotten shoe lying in the path.

Who was this artist? Who was *Suleiman bin Abadi*? Where was he from?

The hack cursed himself for not having brought back more of the young runaway's pictures: missed opportunities.

The hack didn't keep his promise: he didn't go back. Never mind.

Sometimes, to soothe himself, Suleiman drew a face: skin the colour of amber, hair black as a raven's wing. It brought him peace.

Chapter 15

Walking away from the camp, Suleiman realised that he was now alone, homeless and paperless, and his whole body reeked of smoke.

Where now?

After a quick swim in the sea, he stood under one of the cold showers erected along the beach, then he shaved away the thick stubble that had grown around his chin, staring at his image in a small pocket mirror for a long moment, not recognising himself as the same the boy who had run away from his homeland.

With the money Ahmed had split with him and the few euros given to him in exchange for a drawing, he started along the coastal road, not sure where he was heading, his belongings slung over his shoulders.

Finally, an unusually warm spring was slowly and deliberately forcing out the winter cold.

Suleiman gazed up at a sky that was of the clearest pale blue, a few clouds playing aimlessly as gulls screamed and reeled about his head.

He felt a new sense of freedom as he walked, all the while keeping a watchful eye for any spot police checks.

Sometimes he would stop near a seaside café, take out his drawing pad and pencils and draw. People, curious to see, would wander over to watch him sketch a child's portrait.

Some would ask, *'Combien?'* and he would smile and reply, 'Whatever you think it is worth.'

Mothers were always generous, delighted to see their child's face immortalised on paper.

Others preferred to stare, shaking their heads and muttering their disapproval.

He wondered what had happened to Ahmed. He'd seen the newspaper headlines: 'Fire claims at least one victim. Unidentified.' Could it have been Ahmed? But Ahmed was a survivor. Still, he mused, it was unusual for Ahmed not to reappear like a bad djinn. They had been together for so long, sharing so much, that although life without Ahmed seemed almost an improvement, it still felt a little strange with no one to fight, no one to curse.

Life without Layla, though, was unbearably painful.

When he received the text, he had to stop and sit down on the grass verge, staring at the message: 'I am in England.'

He took a deep breath, held it for a few seconds before letting the air out. A grin drew itself across his face. She was safe. May all the gods be praised! He thought he might choke with happiness. He replied immediately.

'Are you well? I miss you. Please tell me where you are and I will come. I will find you. And we will be together.'

'Do you promise?'

The battery warning light came up on his phone.

'How can you doubt?'

If he closed his eyes he could hear her voice, see her eyes that were always full of questions, and he thought that if he were a musician he would compose a song for her.

But he could only draw pictures.

He replied, 'Please tell me where you are.'

He received no reply: his phone was dead.

Chapter 16

Suleiman stood on the opposite side of the road, watching the terrace of the Café de la Plage, where women wearing light coloured dresses and men in open-necked shirts sat beneath blue and white striped parasols, chatting and laughing.

Ice cubes clinked in tall glasses.

Life seemed normal, happy. His heart ached to be like them.

He noticed the waitress: a young girl who appeared to be struggling to keep up with the orders of a few testy customers.

He swallowed hard, pushed back his shoulders, raised his head and crossed over the road, walking past the outside tables to enter the café, conscious of his travel-worn rucksack that threatened to knock over a chair, a glass.

He felt rather than saw the curious stares.

He heard a whispered comment and he flinched. He'd heard worse.

Inside, he saw a woman was standing behind the till: short, dark hair, and an open face.

'Can I help you?' She was smiling as he walked towards her.

'Please, do you have any work for me?' He paused. 'I can do anything.'

The woman did not reply immediately. He thought he had made a mistake. Perhaps he should not have come. He saw her glance over at the waitress who was picking up another tray loaded with sandwiches and drinks to take outside.

'You can trust me,' he ventured, because he thought he recognised the expression on her face.

The waitress stopped for a moment, balancing the tray. She called over, 'He could do the washing up.'

The woman shook her head, sighed and looked across at Suleiman. 'That's Cécile for you, always looking out for herself. The dishwasher's broken and she hates washing-up.'

He held his breath.

She nodded. 'All right. Mind, I can't pay you much.'

She pointed to where he could put down his rucksack and held out her hand. 'I'm the owner. My name is Aude Escoffié. You can call me Aude, everyone else does. What's your name?'

'Suleiman, Madame.'

She asked, he thought almost apologetically, 'Where are you from, Suleiman?' Pause. 'Do you have any papers?'

'I lost them, Madame. Somewhere...'

She nodded slowly. ''Okay, Suleiman. In that case, it would be best if you didn't serve at the tables. Stay inside. I should warn you, though, I don't want any trouble. I wouldn't be able to help you if the police got involved.'

'Thank you, Madame.'

She smiled. 'We're not going to get very far if you insist on calling me Madame!'

In the kitchen, he plunged his hands into the warm, soapy water and started to wash plates, glasses and cutlery that were piled high, as if they had been waiting for him.

He allowed himself to smile: he had a job where no one would get hurt.

That evening, after Cécile had gone home, Aude said, 'Thank you for your help today, Suleiman. It seems you arrived just at the right time!' She went to the till and took out some money and handed it to him.

As he accepted the money, Suleiman looked more closely at Aude: he had already noticed the smile that always seemed to hover over her lips. He thought: perhaps she can only see beautiful things... I should draw her.

'Would you fancy staying on for a few more days? The weather's warming up and it can get pretty hectic here. I know Cécile could do with some help.'

Inwardly he praised God – and Cécile - and he nodded.

Aude pointed to his rucksack. 'Do you have any more stuff?'

He shook his head. He thought she might change her mind because she was studying him carefully, as if considering.

She shrugged.

'Look, there's a spare room upstairs. Cécile used to

sleep up there when it got really busy, but these days she prefers to go home to her parents - they live just outside town. You're more than welcome to use it, if it would help? Unless you have somewhere else...?'

He tried to stop the grin that stretched across his face: he failed. 'Thank you. You are very kind.'

'Come on. I'll show you.'

Later, once he had charged his phone, he texted Layla and waited for a reply. None came.

He sent another message, staring at the phone, willing it to receive a reply.

He prayed as he had never prayed before. If he had done bad things, it wasn't his fault, he'd never meant to hurt anyone. Surely, if there was a god then that god could forgive him, just this once.

A couple of warm weeks drifted by and he began to enjoy the company of the two women.

Aude was kind to him and generous, and Cécile always made him laugh.

A man called Serge, fair-haired and narrow-lipped, came to the café five evenings a week, parking his sports car where everyone could see it and admire it. His clothes were expensive and Suleiman never saw him wear the same pair of shoes twice - Ahmed would have been impressed.

Every time Serge entered the small café he would call out, *'Salut tout le monde!'* And he would raise a hand and smile, but his eyes would slide over Suleiman and instinctively Suleiman would step back into the shadows.

Aude told him they were engaged to be married.

Once, while he was finishing up cleaning the kitchen,

Suleiman heard Serge whisper loudly to Aude, 'What's he still doing here? You checked him out? You know you could get into trouble…'

Suleiman had allowed himself a half-smile as he wiped the chrome taps and folded the dishcloth, because on the other two nights of the week when Serge did not visit, Aude would invite Suleiman into her bed and he accepted because he was lonely and her naked body was warm and inviting. It was not love and it was a silent affair, but she paid him extra for something they both needed: they had an arrangement.

Alone in his room, Suleiman took out the drawings he had once made of a beautiful girl. Stroking the curled edges of the paper, he wished his fingers could make the sitter come to life, but as time passed and the silence from his phone grew, he understood that somehow he had lost Layla.

All he had left was the memory of a hasty moment behind a makeshift shower in a refugee camp, when they had clung to one another as if life itself might desert them.

In his sleep he found her, reaching out to curl his fingers about her hair, stroke her soft skin the colour of warm caramel, kiss her mouth and love her over and over.

Summer sped by and he stayed at the Café de la Plage, working in the kitchen, washing up, cutting vegetables, making sandwiches, and making love twice a week, laughing to himself whenever he saw Serge.

On those evenings, after Cécile had gone home and

before they went upstairs to Aude's bedroom, they would sit in the kitchen drinking coffee or a glass of wine and he would tell her tales from his homeland.

They developed a closeness, although still he kept the veil of secrecy tightly drawn.

After their love-making and back in his room, reality would return and he would take out his money and count it because despite everything, he needed to find Layla.

One night, as they lay naked on the bed, the window open to a velvet sky and a cool night breeze, Aude said to him, 'I'm sorry.' And Suleiman shook his head, 'Why?'

'Serge is very rich,' she hesitated before adding, 'and I am not.'

He took her hand and kissed it. 'It's okay, I understand. It is our secret. He will never know…' He waved his hand above their naked bodies, 'about this.'

He began to enjoy his new life: his friendship with Aude and Cécile, the way they laughed together, the familiar noise of the people sitting outside eating and drinking and happy.

Time sped by.

He started to think he might be able forget…

'Shall I cook for you tonight?' He wanted to repay them for their kindness.

Aude nodded. 'Okay.'

But as he prepared the meal, the warm smells of the cooking, the mint and the lemons and the taste of the olive oil made his head spin.

And as the women ate greedily without seeing his misery, he remembered his homeland, the rivers and the distant snow-capped mountains, the sound of the oud playing, the muezzin calling to prayer from his minaret…

He knew then there were some things he could never forget.

One afternoon Cécile came into the kitchen with a small order.

As he started to prepare a sandwich, she said, 'There's a man outside, Suleiman. He showed me a picture on his phone. He asked if I'd seen you. I didn't know what to say. I just said, I don't think so. He hasn't gone away though. He's still standing there. Creepy.'

He felt the sharp bite of fear as he realised that over the past few months he had become complacent: life had felt easy, gentle.

Cécile touched his arm; she was friendly, always full of energy. He had come to look forward to her smile every morning when she arrived for work.

'Don't look so worried! I didn't say anything and he's definitely nothing official. Trust me, I can tell. He looks more like one of those…' She stopped. 'Oh, I'm sorry, so sorry! I didn't mean…' She continued, turning her flushed cheeks away from him. 'He said he'd wait for you, across the road.'

He smiled with a confidence he did not feel. 'Don't worry. I'll take a look and see if I recognise him.'

He walked slowly towards the open doors of the café, keeping to the shadows.

Outside, he could see the sky was a pale blue, grey clouds were gathering, the sun was losing its warmth. Customers had dwindled, drifting back to the cities and children to their schools.

He looked beyond the few people still sipping their coffee and chatting.

His eyes flicked over the small, stone wall that divided the pedestrian walk from the white, sandy beach, where he would often sit and draw.

That was when he saw him, sitting on the wall, and he felt everything that had happened in the past few months drain away, as the past roared back at him.

Unthinking, he stepped out of the shadows, and the figure waved.

He blinked a few times, not because of the sun which had disappeared, but rather because he did not want to believe what he was seeing.

He began to walk towards the road, each step forward an effort, stopping at the pavement's edge, pretending to wait for the cars to stop before he crossed over.

The figure jumped down from the wall and stood. Waiting.

The shout made him shudder.

'My friend! Suleiman, my friend, where have you been? I have been looking for you. You are hard man to find, my friend.'

The empty word repeated three times in less than a minute.

Suleiman felt the other man's arms hold him in a hug as he was kissed on both cheeks, then Ahmed gripped Suleiman's arm. 'I have missed you! Have you missed me?'

Suleiman swallowed hard. The man who stood in front of him had not changed: the same angry eyes, the taunting grin, the hand-out clothes discarded now for a black leather jacket, another pair of cowboy boots and a baseball cap advertising some American product.

Finally, he asked, 'What happened to you? I thought...'

Ahmed laughed, and Suleiman sensed the laugh did not come from any sense of geniality.

'What did you think had happened to me? Did you perhaps think I'd been burnt alive?'

The two locked eyes.

'Tell me what you were thinking, Suleiman, when you walked away? When you left?' With one hand Ahmed twisted the baseball cap around so the long visor covered his neck, with the other he tightened his grip on Suleiman's arm. 'I tried calling you. Several times. Did you know that? Couldn't get through. Any idea why?'

Suleiman clenched his jaw.

'You didn't block my number did you – by any chance? Because I don't think you went looking for me? What were you hoping? That I'd been reduced to a pile of grey ashes?'

He released his hold and Suleiman staggered backwards.

Ahmed was no longer laughing, his face had turned to a sneer. '*She* got out, though, didn't she? That's loyalty for you. Didn't take you with her.' He stopped. Perhaps realising that this was not the moment. 'Guess you've a lot of questions you want to ask me, my friend. I also have questions, like, what are you doing here?' He pointed at the café across the road. 'Any easy pickings for me?'

Suleiman looked back and saw Cécile shading her eyes with her hand as she watched. 'How'd you find me?'

Ahmed raised open palms and pulled a face. 'Fate or whatever. No point in staying at the camp, there was nothing left and I wasn't going to be shunted about with all those other losers. Thought I'd make my way along the coast.'

So that was it, they'd both had the same idea. He wished Ahmed hadn't stopped here, wished Ahmed had carried on down the coast, wished Ahmed had never found him.

He said, 'I've got a job here. They're nice people. You?'

He asked but he didn't care, he didn't want to know. All he wanted was for Ahmed to go away.

'I've done a bit of work here and there, as long as no questions asked.' Ahmed turned the visor back so it covered his face. 'I fell out with some screwball who said he'd report me if I didn't hand him over some money.' He paused. 'The screwball is no more... so I had to go back on the road and here I am! It was yesterday, I saw you coming out of that café and I thought to myself, that's my friend Suleiman! How amazing is that? What a piece of luck! I recognised you straight away, by the way, despite the shaved beard although, my friend, you have put on some weight! You must be enjoying the good life, no?' He sniggered and nodded towards Cécile, 'Pretty waitress. That how you've forgotten Layla?'

Suleiman could feel his fists itching to slam into the other's face but his feet were willing his body to turn back to the café, willing him to walk away.

'I have to go. Work to do.'

'Don't worry. I can wait here for you. Don't be too

long. We've got lots of catching up to do and, my friend, I've got something you might like to see. I've been keeping it for you. A secret I've decided to share with you, as a friend.'

'Yeah, well see you in a while.' Suleiman walked back to the safety of the café, to the warmth of the kitchen, to the questioning eyes of Aude and Cécile, who had been watching and waiting.

He stood in the kitchen and wondered.

He wondered what the secret was that Ahmed wanted to share. Whatever it was, it wouldn't be anything good.

He wondered how he could explain to these two women who had never questioned him that his world was a very different one to theirs; his was a world where bad things happened; a world where the strongest are always the winners.

In the end, 'I have to go,' was all he said.

'Why?' It was Cécile who asked the simple question. Cécile with her smile that made deep dimples in her cheeks. 'Why must you go?'

'Just, it's time.' What reason could he give? How could he tell them that he was afraid of the man who stood outside; afraid because Ahmed was destructive; because Ahmed reminded him of a past he wanted to forget? Here, in this small café, he had found peace, he had found friendship of a sort, love of a sort. If he stayed, Ahmed would destroy all of that.

Aude reached out and put a hand on his arm. 'It's okay,' she said.

He stared down at the slender fingers that had caressed him two nights a week; he looked at the warm body that had held him close and he thought that if he closed his eyes and opened them again he would see that it had all been a dream.

'It was going to happen sooner or later, wasn't it? Do you know that man outside?'

He nodded. 'He mustn't see me leave.'

Aude turned back to the till and took out the day's takings. 'Take this,' she pushed the money into his hand. 'This should help you for a while.'

He heard Cécile sniff and saw her put a tissue up against her eyes. 'That's really sad,' she said. 'I thought we were friends.'

'Wait a minute,' he fumbled in his rucksack, took out his drawing pad and leafed through it until he found what he was looking for. 'Here,' he said, 'for you. We shall always be friends.'

Cécile caught her breath as she looked at the portrait he had made of her. She was carrying a tray full of empty glasses and plates; her hair was slightly dishevelled and her cheeks were pink and shining; she was wearing a short yellow skirt and a black tee-shirt. She smiled with delight.

'I've signed it,' he said. 'You never know, I may be famous one day.'

Suleiman went over to Aude and held out his arms to her.

She did not move towards him but she nodded. 'I hope you find what you're looking for,' was all she said.

He left the Café de la Plage by the back door as the sun dipped on the horizon, all his belongings once more thrown over his back.

Ahmed was still sitting outside on the wall opposite.

Smoking. Waiting.

Chapter 17

Ahmed sighed and wriggled on the uncomfortable stone wall.

If he had been a betting man which he wasn't, unless it involved human trafficking, he would have placed a bet that Suleiman would not come out of the front of the café opposite to join him.

He muttered to himself, 'Ah, Suleiman, I know you so well, my friend. Trust me, you will never escape me.'

He waited until he saw the pretty little waitress leave, noted that she did not look in his direction and his lips curled. This was proof, if proof were needed, that they had conspired in helping Suleiman to leave by a different way. Why were people so stupid? No matter. He jumped down from the wall, picked up his bag, licked his lips, passed a hand over his dark beard and followed her, watching the early evening breeze play with her yellow skirt.

He caught up with her as she reached a bend in the road that led out of town. The shops had disappeared, the road was empty and on either side were pine trees and sandy paths leading from the road into the woods. Sandy paths where lovers would walk on Sundays.

'Excuse me, Mademoiselle,' he grinned as he caught up with her and she turned. He noted the flicker of unease on her face. 'I wonder if you can help me.'

She slowed down, but she did not stop walking.

'Please, Mademoiselle. Can you stop for a minute?' He allowed his hand to brush against her arm. She pulled away but she stopped.

'What do you want?' Her voice was unfriendly. It amused him.

'My friend, Suleiman, I was waiting for him outside the café back there,' he waved his arm in the direction of the Café de la Plage. 'You do remember me? I showed you his picture. I don't know what can have happened. I've been waiting for so long. Do you know if he's still inside the place? He told me he worked there, and when I saw you coming out...'

'I've no idea.'

She was lying, of course. Perhaps she was secretly in love with Suleiman, just like the other one? No matter.

'You must think me rude and I am sorry to bother you. I mean, look at me: I'm just a refugee from one of the camps. I've lost everything - my family, my home. I have nothing. All I have is in this bag,' he held his bag out in front of him. 'And you see, I had only one friend in the world: Suleiman.'

He watched her waver and he understood what a spider must feel like when it sees a fly venture too close.

'Suleiman and me, we have walked thousands of miles together; we have been shot at, we've watched fellow refugees – friends - die of hunger.' He lowered his voice, pressed fingers over dry eyes. 'We have shared everything.' Although, he thought to himself, not quite everything…

She was shaking her head, staring at him more attentively.

Around the bend came a sports car, the noise of the engine drowning Ahmed's words as the driver pressed the horn and a passenger leaned out, waved and shouted. 'See you tomorrow, Cécile!' And then they were gone even as the girl called Cécile smiled and raised her hand to wave back. Perhaps she had wanted them to stop?

Ahmed saw the way her skirt rose ever so slightly with the lift of her arm; he saw the bare legs; he had already observed the slight marks of perspiration under the arms of her thin cotton blouse. Had Suleiman touched her?

'Nice car,' he said.

The girl's smile was immediately wiped from her face. He liked the way she looked at him: it gave him a sense of power. He nodded his head almost imperceptibly: she was right to fear him.

'Look, please let me explain, so you'll understand.' This time he gripped her arm, and as she resisted he pushed her onto the sandy path and part-pushed, part-carried her further into the pine wood.

'What are you doing? Let go of me!'

Close up, her body felt soft and warm; he could have slung her over his shoulders and walked a thousand miles with her and it would have felt like heaven.

'Please don't struggle. You can see it's pointless. Let's go and have a chat where we will not be disturbed.'

'Let me go, please. I must get home.'

'Shhhhh.'

They were now at some distance from the road. He could hear the odd car drive by but he knew they could not be seen. He looked about several times, put his head to one side, listening for any sound. There was silence; not even a bird song as the cloak of evening fell gently over the tree-tops.

'Do not be afraid, please. So your name is Cécile?'

'Yes.' Her voice was merely a whisper.

'That's nice. Well, Cécile, I just need to explain, so you understand.' He had taken them away from the path and stopped beneath one of the tall trees, pushing Cécile down onto a bed of pine needles.

For a moment he stood looking down at her, sniffing in the sweet, tangy smell of the pine then he sat down beside her.

'You see, there was a fire in the camp where we were, and Suleiman thought I had died. Imagine that? Suleiman, my friend, he thought I had been burnt to death. He must have been horrified, so of course he left the camp. He ran away, if you like, and it seems he stopped off at your café looking for work. I expect you were kind to him?'

The smirk was hidden beneath the beard. 'It is very easy to be kind to Suleiman, isn't it? Were you kind to him? How kind were you?'

'I don't know what you mean. No. He just seemed a nice person. Please, please let me go home. Please don't hurt me. Is it money you want?' As she struggled he caught sight of a drawing inside her open bag.

'He drew your picture! I see he has not lost his talent! This is amazing. You must be very pleased with it? Tell me what you had to do to get this picture? It wasn't free, was it? I know, everybody loves Suleiman. He's such a gentle soul, isn't he?'

He saw her eyes were wide open, her pupils dilated with fear, her breasts heaving with a curious rapidity beneath the blouse and he found himself thinking, 'I loved him too. Pity he couldn't have loved me.' He pushed the thought away.

'You see, I think when he saw me this afternoon, it came as a shock. I must have frightened him. He probably thought I had returned from the dead. A ghost, me! My poor, dear friend. What a thought!'

He pulled out a cigarette and offered one to Cécile; she shook her head and he continued.

'Which is why I must find him. In order to help him. He needs my help.' He added, 'You can trust me.'

He had come to like those two words almost as much as 'my friend.'

Keeping one hand on Cécile's short skirt, he put the cigarette back into his pocket.

'You're right of course. Why spoil our meeting by smoking.' His fingers caressed her naked leg.

'Perhaps you could show me what you did for my friend? Me and Suleiman we have shared much - didn't he tell you?'

Sometime later, he set off on the road to Paris, the portrait of Cécile screwed into a tight ball and thrown onto the ground.

Cécile had told him she thought Suleiman was headed for Paris. Ahmed could have guessed as much. Throwing his rucksack over his shoulder as he began to walk, he gave a smug smile: he had to admit, Suleiman had good taste, although the bastard would need more than good taste once Ahmed caught up with him.

He'd never forgotten the small boy who had thrashed him in the playground all those years ago; he could still feel the humiliation as the other boys laughed at him, wallowing in their dislike of the school bully.

A school bully who, deep down, only wanted to be friends with this strange boy, but did not know how.

It was then that he started to store up hatred for Suleiman, a hatred that nobody could ever quantify.

He despised the way others looked at Suleiman with eager smiles on their faces - so different to the way they looked at him, Ahmed.

Even the refugees did not smile at him, they did not thank him, and yet it was *he* who worked so tirelessly on their behalf, trying to save their stupid, worthless lives. They could always find a smile for Suleiman, a kind word! They would thank Suleiman. Sometimes they even embraced him. Suleiman, a man who was cursed from the day he was born, a man who had not lifted a finger to save his mother and father. A man who drew pictures, for God's sake!

Finally, Ahmed could never forgive the man who had taken from him the one thing he coveted more than anything else.

When he had held Layla in his arms as they struggled in those icy waters, feeling her young limbs beneath her wet clothes as she clung to him he had known, he had understood that she belonged to him, not to that other spineless individual.

Until the evening of the fire, he had believed everything was possible, that somehow he would be able to convince Layla to see reason, to understand how much stronger he was, how he could take care of her. He had imagined she might have the same thoughts about him - until he saw the pair of them emerge from behind the showers, holding hands, still flushed from their moment of union.

Then he had wanted to scream out his hatred because he was too late... Too bloody late...

Even now he could feel the anger, the jealousy welling up inside him. That night he had wanted to rush over and slice Suleiman's throat, separate his head from his shoulders.

He had wanted to take Layla and stone her for what she had done.

Instead, he had run and hidden behind one of the make-shift tents, swearing to get his own back as he swallowed the tears, swearing to hurt them both as much as they had hurt him, by using the one weapon he now had in his possession.

He straightened up now as he walked, watchful, keeping out of sight as much as possible, reasoning that anyone who saw him would think he was just another lazy, good-for-nothing alien and would barely throw him a glance.

He had no fear – he had seen too much - and he had amassed a tidy sum: people smuggling was a lucrative business.

He'd bought himself false papers. He'd baulked at the price they wanted to charge, but in the end he'd made them see reason: the sharp tip of the knife had proved it could be used for more than just peeling apples.

Layla was gone now, out of his reach, only Suleiman

left to pay for what they had done.

Suleiman had deceived him and he had betrayed Allah, and such betrayal came at a very high price.

He slipped his fingers into his inside jacket pocket and fingered an envelope. 'Ah, Suleiman my friend, I have missed you.'

He pulled the visor of his baseball cap further over his face, gathered spittle into his mouth and spat it onto the ground: the tiny bubbles took several moments to disperse.

Chapter 18

'Where you heading?'
 The lorry driver leaned out of the window of his cabin and Suleiman pulled away, afraid.
Trust no one.
He had no idea how long he had been walking: time had no value. He was alone and fear walked with him once again: fear of being stopped, of being found out and now fear that Ahmed might be somewhere behind him.
The driver revved his engine: he was impatient.

Suleiman glanced down at his new trainers that replaced a pair of broken sandals, the soles of which had detached themselves from the body of his shoe as he walked.
He'd managed to carry on for a while, gripping the soles with his toes until he'd reached a village and a small market, where a woman with bright red hair and matching lipstick, standing behind a stall displaying dozens of pairs of trainers, had called out and beckoned to him to come closer.
'*Monsieur*!'
He hesitated, looked around, but she called out to him

again, still beckoning with her hand.

As he approached, she held out a pair of blue and white trainers but he shook his head and backed away, looking down at his broken sandals, the chipped toenails, the dirt.

But the woman insisted, '*Mais si*! Try them, with these.'

With the trainers, she offered him a pair of white socks. 'They should be your size.' She smiled.

Slowly, he bent down and pulled one sock over his foot and then the trainer. It was a good fit. He looked up at the woman and she nodded pointing to his other foot.

When he put his hand into his pocket to pay her, she shook her head: *'Non, ça n'est pas nécessaire.'*

For a moment he stood staring at her, then he walked a few paces, put down his rucksack and took out his pencil and some paper.

He worked quickly.

When he handed her the finished picture, her eyes smiled with delight.

He nodded and smiled back at her, 'I have signed it!'

It felt strange to be sitting in the cabin, next to the driver. Suleiman found himself wondering what was in the back of the lorry. He decided not to ask.

He fell asleep and was awoken a few hours later by the driver's voice.

'Paris,' he said.

Suleiman blinked, not understanding. Paris? Already?

The driver said, 'You get out here. And mind the police,' he warned, and then he waved goodbye and he was gone.

Suleiman stood still for a few moments, not knowing in which direction to walk, overcome by a sudden sense of freedom.

It was the sight of the blue tents that dismayed him. He had not expected to see them here, not in the city: the same small affairs of blue and grey and black, shaped like the shells of snails, all parked haphazardly beneath a fly-over. He'd thought that part of his life was over; it seemed he was still a runaway who did not belong and who was not wanted.

'*Eh! Vous! Arrêtez!* Stop!'

He heard the shout and saw the policeman running towards him.

He turned to run and was knocked over by another man who shouted, '*Poussez-vous*!' and pushed him to one side.

He got up slowly. He gripped his hands together: they were shaking. He heard the sound of the siren as a police van sped by.

The policeman had stopped running and turned away.

For a moment Suleiman stood huddled in a doorway, watching, before he realised the excitement was over and nobody had noticed him.

'You must be new here?' The man was wearing glasses - only one side had a lens. He was completely bald. Through the empty lens Suleiman saw that the eyes carried the tiredness he had seen so many times.

Unsure, Suleiman took a step back. Then he nodded, changed his mind and shook his head.

The man shrugged. 'Ask over there. If you want, they'll give you something to eat and one of those.' He waved in the direction of the tents and Suleiman saw people were queuing where a few volunteers were handing out food, small bottles of water and plastic ponchos.

He moved away from the man who was now holding out an empty, upturned palm.

The volunteers were friendly, offering free advice and help, but always with the same questions:

'Where are you from?

'How old are you?'

'Are you on your own?'

Trust no one... The less said the better.

He accepted the food, the water, the small grey tent, but he was infused with a sense of bewilderment as he followed the lives of these fellow runaways.

He wasn't part of their world. Or was he?

They warned him of the raids: police could arrive at any time in vans euphemistically called *paniers à salade,* round up as many aliens as possible and move them out of Paris.

'But we come back. Always!' One alien shouted joyfully. 'I came back!'

Suleiman wanted to cry out, why am I here? I should be back attending to my goats, walking in the mountains, talking with the imam.

And for a very brief moment he disremembered the drought, the hunger, the shootings, the hangings – and Layla; but only for very brief moment.

He found a discarded easel on a pile of rubbish and bought a few more paints and some paper, finding a familiar comfort in the feel of the paper, the stub of the soft pencil clutched, thumb to the forefinger, guiding his hand.

If anyone offered him food or a drink, he would offer to sketch them.

'For you,' he said, offering the finished article in payment, even though they told him no payment was due.

Still, it made them smile as they received the drawing, studying it closely before placing it carefully into a pocket or a bag.

Sometimes, a mother would emerge from one of the blue snail-like shells holding a child. 'Please, I have seen what you do. Please can you draw a picture of my child?'

And he would stare at the mother, seeing the rubbish and squalor that surrounded her, and he saw the unfathomable love and fear in that mother's eyes and he would want to reach out and comfort her. He never did.

Often he could not understand their language, nor they his: gestures sufficed.

Sometimes they handed him a battered photo of a land left behind long ago, now only a cherished memory. 'Please can you draw this?'

'I cannot pay you.' He heard those words so many times.

'Please. Take it,' he said, because whether he drew for money or not, he couldn't stop drawing.

When he allowed it, his mind drifted back to Aude and the warmth of her bed and of Cécile and her dimpled smiles but not often: those days were part of a tapestry, they were the corner bits that made it up and in the centre was another woman he still dreamt of seeing again.

The shadows were always there, though. Haunting

him.

Every so often he caught sight of a figure he thought he recognised, and he would stand motionless, willing the figure to vanish and when it turned about and stared at him, it was never Ahmed.

Winter advanced in its cold way, and leaves that were once red, gold and yellow were changing to a dirty brown, covering the ground, waiting to be crunched underfoot

Weak rays of sunshine still splashed over hungry, brown sparrows that hopped about scrambling for crumbs.

Today, he felt almost happy as he saw people sitting in the boulevard cafés, drinking their hot chocolate and their cafés crèmes.

He watched the buses rumbling past, heard the impatient honks of taxis, the ringing of a church bell, the sound of running feet, children laughing.

Had anyone asked him why, he would have said that it was because everything appeared so very normal.

'What's your name?'

Despite the cold, Suleiman offered a smile of friendship to the man who sat on a stool, his easel set up near the Pont des Arts, paintbrush in hand as he appeared to concentrate on his work. Tourists walking over the bridge on their way to the Tour Eiffel, stopped to look and admire – but not to buy.

Suleiman walked several paces away. He did not offer his name.

He put his rucksack on the ground and set about

installing his easel and his other materials.

The man had put the question without turning his head. He repeated his question. 'What is your name?'

Finally, Suleiman answered. 'Suleiman.' Again he smiled.

'Where are you from, Suleiman? You are not French?'

Suleiman felt the weak sunlight drain away.

'Are you planning on staying here? Did I invite you?'

Suleiman hesitated, noting the tone of the man's voice: he had heard it before.

He sighed, shook his head, reached down to fold up his easel and put his paints back into his rucksack.

The man had still not turned his head, although he nodded with approval as Suleiman walked wearily away.

Suleiman thought he heard the man say, 'Don't come back.'

That was the day he reached a decision: he would go to the authorities. Explain that he had no identity papers, that he had lost them; give them the name he had used all his life – not the name he had once chosen because he wanted to stay close to Layla.

If he told them where he was from, they would probably send him back. They would not want to keep him here. Then he would no longer need to fear the police roundups; he would no longer need to keep looking over his shoulder, looking for the shadow of Ahmed.

Back in his homeland, perhaps things would be different now? Nothing could be as bad as the life he was now living – could it?

This was not living: alone, friendless, homeless,

barely any money.

He would never be able to find Layla. He knew that now.

He made up his mind.

Standing outside the *Commissariat Central de Police,* his mouth curved to a half smile at the irony of the large sign written above what was apparently the first floor of the austere building: *Hôtel de Police…*

A man in police uniform, wearing a face covering, stood at the entrance directing people into the building. First, though, he asked to see their papers: their identity.

Standing on the opposite side of the pavement, Suleiman watched.

He saw how some people were directed into the building, once they'd answered a few questions and shown paperwork to the conscientious policeman. Others were turned away: instructed to go elsewhere.

A police van turned up. Suddenly more police appeared, standing by, holding guns.

He watched the van disgorge its load of mainly young men, then he saw an old man he thought he'd met once, and who'd told him he couldn't remember where he was from.

The old man had asked Suleiman to draw him a picture of his wife, but when Suleiman asked to meet her, it turned out his wife was dead: drowned somewhere, on some stretch of water - the old man couldn't remember where. Neither could he recall what she looked like. He kept saying that it was too long ago, but that she was very beautiful.

In the end, Suleiman had drawn a picture of Layla, and as he handed it to the man, the man had nodded and smiled with gratitude, and put the picture inside his shirt, close to his heart.

Now, he saw the old man climb out of the van, look hesitantly to the left and to the right, before a masked policeman took his arm and guided him inside the building with the others.

Suleiman turned away.

Late one afternoon, he went back to his favourite place. A place where people were friendly, where he did not feel an alien, where other artists would come and comment on his work and exchange ideas.

He climbed the two hundred and twenty two steps up to Montmartre.

Positioning himself near to the top of the stone steps, the view of the city behind him, he began to sketch the portrait of a little girl with unruly, fair hair.

Her mother stood by, looking from the sketch to the child and back again, her face anxious.

The child was wearing a dark blue coat with red buttons and a small fur collar. She had a cheeky smile and her young voice was a steady chatter of nothing important.

He smiled as he tried to capture her innocence.

'Will you be able to add colour?' the mother asked.

He pointed to the paints set out in front of him. 'One moment, please.'

He enjoyed applying the colour, watching the portrait come alive. The child's hair was long, and the slight breeze caught at it and played with long wisps that drifted over her head, like a halo.

Behind her, a few remaining leaves that had been

clinging to the branches of a plane tree fell, dancing to the music of the breeze.

Suleiman felt rather than saw the man approach.

He sensed the man's presence behind him. He thought, this must be child's father.

He continued with the portrait, but he had become alert and ready to run.

Once he had finished, he turned to the mother who smiled with delight.

He removed the portrait from the easel and handed it to her.

'Oh, merci,' she said, pulling out a few notes from her purse. 'C'est vraiment très beau.'

The child was already pulling on her hand to go as the man moved forward, and Suleiman felt a twinge of unease as he realised he was not with the woman.

'I've been watching you.' The man was tall, he wore a pair of smart blue jeans, a plain white tee-shirt and a black scarf beneath a brown jacket. His smile was engaging, fair hair tied neatly back from his face.

'I like your work,' he said. 'It's good. Do you have any more I could see?'

Suleiman shook his head, wary: he'd had this conversation before. He threw back his shoulders, his mouth tightened.

'I understand if you don't want to show me.' The man held out his hand. 'The name's Jean-Louis Barre, by the way. Call me Jean-Louis. When you've finished here, and if you change your mind, I'll be sitting outside the café over there.' He motioned with his head. 'Come and have a drink with me.' His mouth stretched to a grin. 'What have you got to lose?'

Suleiman watched the man walk away.

Someone else had once asked him that same question...

Slowly, he folded the easel, put away the pencils, pens, brushes and paints, picked up the folded blue tent, then he pulled himself upright and turned to stare at the café opposite.

The light was waning: evening.

He saw that the man called Jean-Louis was seated outside, beneath an outdoor heater. He was waving, indicating the chair opposite him.

'Thanks for joining me,' he said as Suleiman came over, still hesitant. 'You're not from hereabouts are you?'

Suleiman stood staring, unsure.

'Sorry. Stupid question. Please don't look so worried. I'm not the police or immigration or anything. Please sit down. Coffee?'

Suleiman sat on the edge of the mint green café chair. He had still not spoken. He nodded.

Jean-Louis ordered some coffee for them both before speaking again. 'Would you agree to show me more of your work?' He paused, 'I've been observing you for a while.' He paused again, 'Your work is exceptional. Did you know?'

Suleiman shook his head as his heart skipped one small beat: nobody had ever described his work as exceptional.

Jean-Louis looked through each piece Suleiman offered him, studying every detail, asking questions, 'Where did you do this? Who is that? How long ago...?'

Suleiman answered the questions with caution: he had

been flattered once before, for a fistful of euros.

Once he said to Suleiman, 'Your French is good – where did you learn it?'

'Here and there.' It was enough.

Once, Jean-Louis stared more closely at a painting. He was holding one of the many pictures of Layla, her dark curls falling across bare shoulders, a single tear escaping the corner of her eye.

In his mind, Suleiman had imagined her sitting in a round, rattan cocoon chair, gazing out across a burning landscape, the shadow of a man standing behind her, his face obscured.

'That is beautiful. You did this? It's remarkable. Who is she, the woman?'

'Layla.' As he spoke Suleiman realised it had been a long time since he had said her name out loud. It felt good. He said it again. 'Layla. She is someone I used to know.'

'And the man? The one in the background?'

'No-one.'

'I apologise. I ask too many questions.' He smiled. 'I just like talking to people. You must miss your family? Your home?' Jean-Louis stopped. 'There I go again! Sorry.' And he pushed behind his ear lazy strands of fair hair. 'Tell you what. Why don't we carry on this very one-sided conversation over a meal? Then you can ask *me* questions. Come on. I won't stand for an argument.'

They walked across the cobbled street and Jean-Louis paused as he pushed open the door to a small bistro. 'I'm curious. I presume you sell your work wherever you can in Paris? Tell me, have you ever sold anything online for example? Over the internet?'

Standing on the threshold, Suleiman did not hear the words, did not reply to the question. As soon as the door opened he had felt instant warmth envelop him, his nose quivered at the different aromas; his eyes took in the red leather banquettes, the white tablecloths, the gilt-edged mirrors; his ears heard the humming of people's voices, the clatter of knives and forks, bottles knocking against glasses.

And for a moment he felt intoxicated, his feet holding him back, not wanting to move.

In the end, Jean-Louis took him by the arm and guided him to one of the tables, handing the rucksack, the easel and the folded blue tent to a waiter dressed in a white jacket and black trousers.

He would never be able to remember exactly what they ate and drank that evening.

He recalled Jean-Louis asking him what he would like, but he had felt such a wave of appeasement drift over him, that all he could do was nod at anything Jean-Louis suggested.

'What about *steak au poivre* with *frites*? Although the filet mignon here is…' And he put his thumb and two fingers up to his lips and blew a kiss. Then he said, 'They do an excellent couscous dish as well, with lemon and all sorts. Perhaps you'd prefer?'

Suleiman's mouth spread to a wide grin. 'No disrespect, but I, too, can cook an excellent couscous… with lamb and lemons, currants, cinnamon, saffron, chick peas cooked in a tomato sauce…' he stopped as he felt his cheeks blush with embarrassment, and Jean-Louis laughed and placed an arm behind Suleiman, along the back of the banquette.

As Suleiman listened to Jean-Louis's soft drawl, he wished he could take out his pencil and paper and draw him. Jean-Louis had a way with him, a gentleness, almost a sort of indolence.

When the waiter brought their order: steaks with pepper sauce and chips, Suleiman ate so quickly Jean-Louis asked the waiter for another plate of chips, and Suleiman blushed again. The waiter smiled. Tonight, it seemed that everyone was smiling and he felt as if a weight had, for that moment, fallen from him, all fear gone, evaporated, and as he talked he came to realise he had almost forgotten how to laugh.

'Tell me, where did you learn to draw like that, Suleiman?'

'An imam taught me.'

'Well, he must have been some artist.'

'No, he wasn't an artist, just a good man.'

'Surely you had some formal training? You must have...?'

'I used to look after goats on a mountain side. I'd draw them.'

'You were a goat herd?' Jean-Louis gazed thoughtfully into his glass of red wine, swirling the drink around in the glass. 'That's incredible. I mean the way you use space and colour. Surely, someone must have taught you?'

Suleiman shook his head, frowning because he still did not understand why this man was so interested.

'I have seen the work of a lot of artists, but yours is different. It's raw, as if you've put your own soul into some of those pictures.'

Later, the waiter brought them two double espressos and Suleiman felt Jean-Louis' eyes upon him as he stirred in four lumps of white sugar.

'Look, Suleiman, I asked you earlier, apart from what you sell here, have you ever sold anything elsewhere, I mean, online for example. The internet?'

Suleiman shook his head.

'Your art has a uniqueness. It has drama.'

The recollection of words spoken by another, in what seemed a different lifetime. He did not reply.

'Suleiman, I've got an art gallery just around the corner from here. I'm really impressed with your work. I'd like you to come to my gallery tomorrow, if you can? I want to show you something which I think might interest you.' He looked down at his watch. 'It's getting late. I should be going. Here's my card.' He handed Suleiman a small business card. 'Everyone around here knows me. If you can't find me, just ask. Someone will know.'

They stood outside on the pavement, the cold air in their faces, the warmth of the bistro behind them.

Jean-Louis extended his hand. 'See you tomorrow, then? Eleven o'clock suit you?'

Suleiman nodded. 'Thank you for this evening. That was really kind.' He wanted to say, 'That was the best evening I have ever had in my entire life.' He didn't.

'Not at all. Don't forget, tomorrow.' Jean-Louis turned and Suleiman watched him disappear down the cobbled street, past the cafés and the closed souvenir shops. He swallowed hard.

It was late, and he needed to find somewhere safe to bed down for the night. He threw the rucksack and the tent over his back and began to walk in the opposite direction, keeping away from the street lights, on the lookout for a hidden corner.

There was the sound of running feet and his first thought was that the police had finally caught up with him. He was about to run when he heard a voice call out, 'Suleiman! Stop!'

It is Jean-Louis. 'I am so sorry. Please forgive me.'

Suleiman stared, frowning, as Jean-Louis stood in front of him, panting. 'I never thought... that was so stupid of me. You don't have anywhere to stay do you?' He pointed to the folded blue tent on Suleiman's shoulder.

That was the evening Suleiman finally saw his life turn one thousand degrees in a different direction, the evening when he started to believe that there was a god after all, when he started to believe that perhaps he would find Layla.

Chapter 19

Next morning, at eleven o'clock precisely, Suleiman stood outside the art gallery, gazing at the paintings in the window.

Inside, everything looked so clean and modern, from the shiny wooden floor to the paintings on display.

Jean-Louis invited Suleiman into his upstairs office where a glass balcony overlooked the gallery below. 'Did you sleep well last night?'

'Yes. Thank you, thank you.' He said it twice because he thought it sounded more sincere. He looked around him, at the highly polished desk, at the man sitting in the black leather chair in front of a computer screen that had been pushed to one side, at the white walls covered with colourful prints of Paris and Provence.

'I've brought my things with me. I've left the place tidy.' He spoke earnestly.

The other leaned back and laughed and to Suleiman's ears the laughter was warm.

'If you agree to my terms here at the Gallery, the apartment's yours for as long as it takes.'

'I cannot afford…'

'It's empty at the moment. You'd be doing me a favour.'

Suleiman wanted to get up and leave because, he thought, here we go… it's going to be another deal like one of Ahmed's, or that two-faced hack. I'm going to be screwed all over again.

He asked, 'What do you mean by "terms"?'

'First of all, I need to ask you something.' Jean-Louis placed his hands, palms down, on the desk. 'When I saw your work, it reminded me of something I saw on the internet some time ago. Can I show you?'

Suleiman shrugged. 'Sure.'

'Come round here. Sit next to me.' Jean-Louis pulled a chair near to him and motioned to Suleiman. He moved the computer screen so they could both see. He tapped a few keys and suddenly there was a picture on the screen that Suleiman recognised.

'Does that look familiar?'

'Wow!' Suleiman peered more closely at the screen. 'That's amazing! How did you find it? Yes, yes of course, it's one of mine. I did it a while back and…' He stopped, because he was remembering the camp, he was remembering the fire, people running, people screaming, Layla and Ahmed and finally he remembered the hack.

'You did sell it though?'

'Yes, sure. For a couple of euros. It was to some guy, said he was a journalist.'

'Tell me what happened.'

After Suleiman had explained, Jean-Louis asked him, 'Can I show you a bit more?' And he tapped a few more keys and the selling price of the picture came up on the screen.

Suleiman stared in disbelief. 'What? That can't be possible. I don't understand…'

'Your journalist bought it from you, and then sold it online.'

'But… so much. How? I still don't understand.'

'It happens. I guess he was at the right place at the right time. Besides, the fire, the camp, all those people, it was an appalling disaster. Everyone heard about it; everyone felt sorry for the refugees - for you. Everyone felt guilty. And someone obviously wanted to purchase their own piece of the tragedy. To hold and to keep.' He smiled. 'Now that we have established that, can we talk business?'

Suleiman said, 'You should know that I am cursed. Bad things happen to me.'

'Cursed?'

Suleiman twisted his mouth. 'It was something I was always told when I was a child.'

'Sounds grim. Anyway, I don't believe in curses.'

When Suleiman got back to the apartment, he took out the advance payment Jean-Louis had given him for two pictures to be framed and exhibited in the gallery.

'I know a lot of important people, wealthy people. You'll see. I'll make sure we get your papers sorted. It won't be a problem. Then you'll be a free man.'

Suleiman spread the bank notes out on the bed and counted them again and again. He had never dreamt of having so much money and it was his, all of it. Now, he could find Layla; marry Layla.

He picked up his phone and checked for messages, as he checked every day: nothing.

He stretched himself out on the bed and closed his

eyes and slept.

Chapter 20

Finally, he was legal. It had taken over a year but Jean-Louis had all the right connections. It felt strange to hold the document in his hands for the very first time; to look down at his photo and see his name and his signature stamped across it.

'Happy?'

Suleiman took the document from Jean-Louis' extended hand.

Jean-Louis was still grinning and Suleiman could think of nothing to say that would explain the sense of relief it gave him to hold that document: the sudden release from the constant fear of the unknown that had pursued him for so long.

He breathed in deeply and exhaled several times, then he held out his hand and smiled. '*Merci, mon ami.*'

And the other opened his arms and they hugged.

Afterwards, his sudden place in the spotlight was speedy, vertiginous almost. To Suleiman, it made no sense that he, a goat herd, a man who did not even know who his real parents were, should suddenly have become a person of such interest to so many. It seemed everyone wanted to crawl through every corner of his life: where was he from, where had he learnt his skills, what were his qualifications, who were his parents, where were his parents now?

He had nothing to tell: he had left his past behind.

He was able to move into a fully-furnished, top-floor apartment in a bustling part of the city, not far from the gallery. The apartment had tall windows that looked over the rooftops of Paris, reaching almost from the dark wooden floors to the high, white ceiling.

Out of his memory box leapt the picture of another house, in another country: the house where Layla had lived; the house with its broken mosaic floors and wide, broken staircase; the high walls lined with paintings of Arabs astride white stallions, gazing down with contempt at the mortals below.

He remembered the promise he had made. '*One day, I will paint like that.*'

His work was now on permanent display at Jean-Louis' gallery; it was becoming recognised within art circles. Jean-Louis suggested they host a cocktail party.

'I have a number of wealthy clients. I'll invite them - get them to come for a private viewing of your paintings. I want people to understand what lies behind so much of your work.' He grinned. 'And I need them to part with some of their money!'

Suleiman looked out at the grey sky from his apartment window and thanked whatever god was watching over him. Never before had he dreamt of having so much money at his disposal and it felt faintly disquieting, as if he were treading on the corpses of all those he had walked with, not so long ago.

It was the evening of the private viewing and he stood on the threshold of a new world, gazing up at his work hanging on the white walls, vibrant colours forcing the viewer to step back and take in every stroke of the brush, every form and shadow.

He stared in awe at what Jean-Louis had accomplished, setting paintings that had seemed almost oversized in huge frames, lighting them from above or from below.

In one corner of the room he saw a painting he had told Jean-Louis he would never sell; it was that of a young girl wearing a torn yellow dress sitting on an upturned box, small fingers clasping the string tied around a child's balloon, her face turned slightly sideways as she watched a fire consume what looked like the remnants of a ramshackle camp behind her.

'What do you think?'

Suleiman shook his head.

'What? You don't like it?'

'My friend,' and Suleiman leant on the two words with great gentleness, 'it is truly amazing. I cannot believe it. These are all my paintings? How can I ever thank you?' And in his heart he wanted to cry with joy, but he couldn't.

'No need. Here, have a glass of this.' Jean-Louis took a glass of champagne from a tray held by a passing waiter and handed it to him. 'This is your night, Suleiman. Enjoy it. Tonight you will become even more famous. And, if we're lucky, you will become richer than you could ever have believed possible.'

Slowly sipping the unfamiliar drink, Suleiman watched the guests beginning to drift in through the glass doors, coming in from the chill night air into the warmth of the golden lights. Women in cocktail dresses cut low to reveal white flesh or skin of polished walnut, their hands draped over the arms of men in velvet jackets worn over immaculate white shirts.

Everyone smiling. Friendly.

Everyone excited and hoping to spend money.

As the room filled, Suleiman felt the air become heady as perfumes wafted and blended. The chatter and the laughter rose and he shook his head in faint disbelief as he watched people use magnifying glasses to study his work in greater detail.

A piece of him wanted to turn and leave because he realised that somehow he had lost his way. He was no longer an artist, he was an investment, something people wanted to own. He felt lightheaded. All he could see were people on the lookout for new talent to bring them more money, as if they did not have enough already.

He was still holding his glass of champagne and wondering if Jean-Louis would ever forgive him if he left, when there she was: a slim, willow of a woman, one arm poised on that of a thick set, bear of a man, who breathed heavily as he displayed his possession.

For an instant, the crowds parted and she stood alone, like a dancer abandoned on a stage. Then the crowds moved urgently towards the couple and she smiled greetings. She wore a long, scarlet evening dress with a high neck and threads of gold running through it. Her only jewellery a pair of diamond ear rings which caught at the light as she moved her head. Short curls formed a frame around delicate features.

A scent of affluence surrounded the couple.

People stood aside to let them pass, whispering amongst themselves: wealth can create a secret jealousy.

'Suleiman, allow me to introduce my very good friend, Monsieur Nabil Assadi and his charming wife.'

It was embarrassing that the wife of one of Jean-Louis' main clients should have fainted. Perhaps it was the warmth of the gallery after the chill outside; perhaps she had not been feeling well.

Suleiman thought he must be having a heart-attack: his heart was pounding so loudly he could feel it in his ears; his feet refused to move from the spot as he stood staring down at the woman stretched out on the floor, droplets of golden liquid slipping down the scarlet dress.

'Quick! Somebody please call my chauffeur.' The heavy-set man bent down to help his wife.

He heard Jean-Louis. 'Help, Suleiman, come on man! Move yourself. Help get her onto a chair.'

One of the waiters went out to call for the chauffeur. A chair was brought.

Suleiman bent down to help the young woman; her husband pushed him to one side.

'Please do not touch my wife.' With great care, Mr Assadi gathered his wife in his arms and carried her to the waiting car as Jean-Louis followed him, repeating several times, 'I am so sorry, Monsieur Assadi.'

Before climbing into the car after his wife, the bear of a man turned to shake his head. 'This is not your fault, Jean-Louis. My wife's health has always been fragile. These things happen.' And then the car melted away into the traffic, red tail-lights mingling with the other cars.

Inside the gallery, Suleiman had to stop himself from shaking. People were milling about once more, discussing what had happened.

Suleiman wondered if his eyes had played tricks on him. His hand was still shaking as he brought another glass of champagne to his lips and poured the sparkling liquid down his throat.

Then he went to refill his glass.

Chapter 21

She felt her husband's strong arms carry her to the waiting car; she opened her eyes and saw him looking down at her, anxious.

'My love, are you alright? Tell me.'

'What happened?'

'You fainted.'

And then it came back to her as if she had been hit by a wall of ice. She shivered, allowing her body to fall back onto the car seats as a rug was placed over her legs.

'Home.' Her husband directed the driver and he took her hand in his large paw. 'We will make sure you see a doctor tomorrow.'

'No, please. It was so warm in there and it is quite chilly outside.' She shivered again. 'My body couldn't take the change in temperature.'

He nodded, and she noticed how the streetlights reached through the car windows and shone on his white hair.

She closed her eyes.

She began to drift.

She began to remember what she had so often tried to

forget.

It seemed a lifetime ago since she left that camp in northern France and reached England and the home of her aunt and uncle, scared and angry, ill-fitting clothes hanging over her thin shoulders.

She remembered the grey English sky, the chilly sea mist that had hovered mid-air as the ship came into the harbour.

She remembered the white gulls screaming and diving into the grey waters as if they wanted to chase her away.

That first night, when she had finally been left alone, she had stood under the hot shower and scrubbed her skin as if to rip it away, anything to rid herself of the stench and the dirt of the camp. But she couldn't scrub away the memory of her dear Baba, of her sisters who had never returned home, of Moonif waving a gnarled hand as she walked away with two strangers.

The water and the soap couldn't wash away the memory of the explosions, of the permanent fear, of the hunger.

Beneath closed eyelids she could still see Ahmed and his cruel smile and, standing a little behind him, Suleiman.

And a wave of anger overcame her because Suleiman had not waited, had not been there to hold her hand, to whisper to her that all would be well, to stand by her, to protect her.

Her aunt and uncle were kind but she knew that they could never understand what she had gone through.

Those first days and weeks, people came by the

house, offering help, trying to comfort her, offer her advice, to tell her she must start to live again…

What did they know?

The long days and the long nights with no-one to talk to. No-one who could understand. No-one to wipe away her tears.

She felt as if she were living in a vortex, an invisible, whirling mass pulling her down.

Then came the unexpected arrival of Nabil.

Nabil, invited by her family to come and meet her.

As soon as he entered the room, his large frame imposed itself; his powerful face smothered by a dark beard, giant hands that clasped her small ones in his own. It was as if he were capable of driving out the darkness.

'So this is the niece you have been hiding from us all this time, Dalila.'

Layla blushed and her aunt seemed pleased.

'He is a good man, Layla.' Her aunt entered her bedroom and sat on the edge of the bed and Layla remembered how alarmed she had been, as she stared at her aunt, trying to understand.

'He is a good man and he is also a very wealthy man. It will be a good match.'

As the reality dawned on her, she wanted to shout out, 'But I don't love him. And he is old, too old.'

She went to bed and sobbed herself to sleep, awakening the next morning to find her pillow wet with her tears.

Sobbing this time not because of all that she had left behind, not because she missed her father and sisters: it wasn't her father and sisters that she missed: it was her monthly cycle. She kept saying to herself that it was not possible, that she would start to bleed soon.

She prayed to any god that would listen, whispering that it was unfair and how could it be? She had given herself to one man only, once in her entire, short life, surely, surely it could not be?

When she missed the following month, panic moved out and dread moved in.

Her aunt took away her phone, despite her protestations.

'I need my phone. Please auntie. What if my friends try to reach me? Please, I'm begging you.'

Her aunt shook her head and walked out of the room, holding the phone. 'You have a new life here now, Layla,' she said. 'New friends.'

One afternoon, when the rain outside was throwing itself against the windows as if demanding entry, she opened up the folded picture frame containing the photograph of her Mama next to the lock of hair.

'This is your Mama?' Nabil asked, a wide finger gently stroking the picture.

'Yes.' And she stopped, closing her eyes for a moment. She had started to find a kind of peace in this house, to accept this older man who came every day to see her, who was kind, who was gentle. This man who was so easy to talk to… this man she was about to deceive.

'The lock of hair is yours?'

She stared down at the dark curl encased within the small picture frame.

'No, not mine.' Fragments of conversations

overheard a long time ago came back to her, but they were rumours, weren't they? Gossip. Her Baba had said so, forbade her to listen.

'My Baba said it belonged to a baby my mother loved and lost.' She stopped for a moment. 'He cried when he told us, but it was before I was born, so I never knew…'

'I am so sorry. But you have experienced a terrifying journey. One day, perhaps, you will tell me what happened to you?'

For a moment the knot in her stomach tightened so hard she gasped. She knew she had to speak up now. There was no time.

His dark eyes were smiling at her.

She turned her face away. 'There is so much that I want to forget, but I cannot.'

'Can you tell me?'

'I never wanted to leave, you know. I was so scared. I remember shouting at Moonif, our gardener.'

She let her voice spin along, her breath becoming shorter and quicker.

'Moonif always seemed so old to me and my sisters. When we were little we would visit him and he'd sit us down in the shade and bring us sweet tea with honey or sometimes fresh juice. He would tell us stories and make us laugh and cry. With my sisters we would run around the garden playing hide and seek, playing ball.'

She pulled a face.

'They were happy days. But I was unkind to Moonif. Before I left, he gave me some seeds. He put them into a little hessian bag and he told me to plant them when I got to England, because he said that would remind me of my home.'

She allowed tears to spill over and slip down her cheeks as she repeated the words, 'My home. My family... where are they now? Why am I the only one left? Why?'

She wanted to howl with the pain of the memories.

'You poor child. But you are here now.' There was compassion in his voice. 'You are safe. I could never imagine how terrible that journey must have been - what you went through. And you, such a young girl.'

'It's really difficult... difficult to talk, to explain.'

He reached out and took her small hand in his. 'Try. Try to tell me,'

'There were men with guns, they would shoot you on sight if they didn't like the look of you and the noise, the pounding... It never stopped. We saw houses that had been hit, destroyed. My own home...'

She gave a small laugh. 'It was almost funny to see armchairs hanging over balconies, sort of suspended in mid-air. But those were armchairs that people had sat in, people who had lived, had children, partied...' She whispered, 'Just ordinary people.'

'Please Layla. If you would rather not talk about it.'

But she wasn't able to stop. It was pouring out. Everything. At the end, of course, there would be the lie, but she had to explain first, so he would understand about the hunger, the omnipresent smell of death and the dying; the donkeys swaying haphazardly before collapsing with exhaustion, their loads tumbling onto the dry earth. Children searching for their parents. Mothers searching for their children. All of them crying, always crying.

And Ahmed goading her, calling her 'princess', telling her to cover her face; Ahmed with his bad teeth, his beard, his threats, his filthy hands. Ahmed, who sometimes made her laugh, even so…

Then she remembered Suleiman and her tears ran faster because, in the end, Suleiman had not been there for her despite all his promises. Gentle Suleiman, who had never tried to find her.

Because of Suleiman she had to lie to this man who sat next to her, holding her hand, shaking his head in horror at what she was telling him.

'And then there were the camps. The horrid, hateful camps. You cannot believe all the dirt, the horrid food, the noise - and the nights…'

She stopped for a moment to look down at the floor, noticing the carpet, the pattern that reminded her of home, seeing as if for the first time the places where it was worn out from foot tread.

She took a short breath.

'There were always bad men circling, looking only for one thing. Some of the women warned me, but I was a fool. I was arrogant. I never thought it could happen to me. Then, one night, I needed to find the toilet badly and one of them, one of the men, followed me. He must have been waiting for me.'

She let the tears of shame roll down her cheeks.

'He…'

She choked then, because she saw Nabil frown and a moment of fear gripped her: now he will get up and walk away. Now he will no longer wish to know me.

'Tell me what happened.' He spoke slowly.

She shook her head. 'I don't think I can.'

'When was this?'

'The night before I came here, the night before I came

to England. I'm so sorry.' She stopped. She felt nauseous, but there was no turning back.

'I am carrying a child.'

As she pushed the words out of her mouth, she placed a protective hand over her abdomen: nothing to show yet.

'Dear God', she prayed, 'please don't ask me to get rid of it. It is all I have left of Suleiman'.

He looked stunned. 'Do you know who the man was?'

'It was dark. He put a hand over my mouth so I could not scream. He kept his face turned from me. He was a big man. I couldn't fight him. He was strong.'

And she stuffed a handkerchief over her mouth to stop herself from being sick as the crimson colour of shame rose from her feet to her high cheekbones.

'Did you not report it? Surely... You must have told someone?'

'Who would have believed me? And if the police had come, what then? They might have stopped me from going to England, they might have kept me at the camp and I would have died if they'd kept me there one more night. You don't understand. I was so scared.' Her voice was thin. 'No-one can understand... '

Somewhere in the house a clock chimed, a door slammed.

She had already become accustomed to his slow, almost ponderous ways and, out of the tail of her eye, she watched him sit in silence, large head bowed, deep in thought.

She wanted to get up and run away. She couldn't.

When, finally, he lifted his head and his eyes stared straight into hers, she wondered if he believed her.

'Layla, listen to me.' As he spoke, he took hold of her

hand and he kissed it. 'I should like you to become my wife, if you will accept me as the father of your child.'

Her aunt cried out in delight - but also in despair: wedding celebrations took time to organise! She could not possibly have everything ready in time. Why the rush? What about the dress? The wedding lunch? The musicians? So much to organise.

And Nabil laughed and took Layla into his arms. 'We are in love! We cannot wait so long,' he cried.

It was on their wedding night that she learnt his truth.

'Layla, I have a secret, too. Perhaps I should have shared it with you before you accepted to become my wife.'

She sat on the edge of a French chair in the vast bedroom with its curtains of heavy green and gold damask and silk carpets, watching the man who was now her husband, as she came to realise that she had now said goodbye to Suleiman for ever.

'I shall not be sharing this bed with you.'

She had been at first relieved, then hurt: was she not good enough for him? Or did he look upon her as damaged goods, as she had once heard someone whisper?

He took her hand and twisted her wedding band round and round with his strong fingers.

'You see, Layla, my tastes lie elsewhere. You are my wife and I will always respect and honour you. Anything you want you shall have. I have promised to be a true father to the child and in return I ask that you never criticise me, never talk of me behind my back. You will understand me in the same way that, I think, I have understood you.'

During the few seconds that followed, she felt her lie scrawl itself across her face.

'And you will never, ever share your body with another man. Do you understand?'

It was the first and only time she ever saw a streak of ruthlessness flash in his dark brown eyes.

She nodded.

'Thank you. Do not ever cross me over this, Layla. It is understood, then?'

Again, she nodded.

So it was that she came to ignore the handsome young boys who visited their large house, and who she would sometimes discover lounging on one of the wide balconies, smoking, listening to loud music, at times smiling at her insolently, at others affably.

She came to ignore the expensive trinkets they flaunted, all gifts from her husband.

She accepted to be at her husband's side on every occasion, smiling up at him as he wrapped her small hand about his arm.

And as Nabil had foreseen, the birth of the child dismissed any gossip regarding his manhood, and the child was feted and Nabil kept his promise - and for that there was no price.

Now, from the depths of her handbag her phone beeped.

Chapter 22

'The woman, who is she? What's her name?'

He could not catch his breath and he sensed rather than heard the slight tremor in his voice as he followed Jean-Louis back into the gallery, after they had both watched the tail lights of the car disappear into the traffic.

Jean-Louis stopped to stare at Suleiman without replying directly to his question. 'What a nightmare!' He put a hand up to his forehead. 'I hope she's going to be okay. Her husband's one of my wealthiest clients. They're a decent couple. I like them. I mean... Why do you think she fainted?' He pulled a face. 'I was hoping he'd buy at least one of your paintings tonight. I'll call him tomorrow.'

'The woman... I think I know her.'

'Look, I need to talk to people here, try and explain.' Already Jean-Louis was moving away from him. 'We can talk later.'

Suleiman felt a prickling sensation on the nape of his neck. He couldn't stop the anger from rising and for one beat of the eyelid he lost control and grasped hold of

Jean-Louis' shoulder.

'I want to know who she is, where she lives and I want to know *now*.'

He saw Jean-Louis's eyes flicker with shock, and he was reminded of the time he had punched Ahmed in the face. Immediately, he released his hold, stepping back, covering his mouth with his hand.

'I'm sorry. I'm sorry.' He repeated the empty words. 'I just want to know... she looks so much like... she reminds me of someone...' His brain felt as if it were tied up in knots and he was trying to sort out the threads. 'I thought she was in England. She never replied to my messages. I stopped trying. And all the while...'

Jean-Louis bit his lower lip. 'Her name is Layla.' He stopped a moment as though some sort of realisation had dawned, although he made no comment.

'She married Nabil Assadi a while back. Not sure when. They used to live in London, but now they live here, in Paris. That's all I know. That's all I can tell you. Now, if you don't mind I'd like to speak with our other guests. After all, it is in your interest as well as mine that we sell a few paintings tonight.'

'Please Jean-Louis, just give me her phone number, if you've got it. That's all. Please.' Because, he thought, she must have changed it, what other reason could there be for her silence? Jean-Louis must have got it wrong: she couldn't be married, that wasn't possible. She'd be waiting for him - wouldn't she? Maybe it wasn't her after all.

Jean-Louis sighed took out his phone and pressed a few buttons.

'Whatever you're playing at Suleiman, be careful.

Nabil's a powerful man.'

Suleiman went back outside and lit a cigarette. He inhaled deeply then dropped it to the floor and squashed it beneath his new, shiny black shoe.

He sent a message to the number Jean-Louis had sent him.

'Did I see you this evening? Was it really you?'

Chapter 23

'Layla?'
She was standing in his doorway, tall, elegant, dressed in white trousers and a pale blue and white cotton mesh sweater. Her eyes were unsmiling.

Her beauty caught his breath. There was a softness about her that had not been there before.

He wanted to throw open his arms, to hold her gently in an embrace, just like he had done all that time ago, behind some shower units in a makeshift camp.

'Come in. Please.' He held out his hand, and his smile extended across his face reaching his eyes, because he wanted to laugh with joy.

'I mustn't stay. I have a car waiting for me.'

He was so intent on looking at her, disbelieving, that he did not hear her words.

He barely heard the quiver in her voice and he did not hear her say, 'My chauffeur is waiting. I...' because he had pulled her gently inside.

'Here, let me take your coat.'

His arms wanted to enfold her, but he dared not. Not yet.

He closed his eyes and breathed in her perfume repeating her name, 'Layla, Layla, I can't believe it! After all this time. I thought I'd lost you forever... and then, the other evening... I found you. At last!'

She held up her hand to stop him, and her tone was bitter.

'No Suleiman, you did not find me. I walked into a room and fate took a hand. You never came to find me in England. I waited until I could wait no longer.'

'I called you. I swear to you. I sent you messages. You only replied once. You never told me where you were. I had no money, no papers. How can you say I didn't look for you? I swear to you... I would have come had you replied. Why didn't you call me and tell me?'

'My aunt took away my phone. She thought it was to protect me.'

'You've got a phone now? You could have tried to reach me.'

'Things changed, Suleiman. I had to make promises you wouldn't understand.'

Still not daring to touch her, he motioned her to the sofa and watched her sit on the very edge, ready to escape.

'So you didn't get my messages? None of them?'

She whispered and he could barely hear her words. 'Some of them, before my aunt took my phone away. You kept asking me: "Where are you? Tell me where you are and I will come."'

'So, why Layla? Why? Why didn't you answer? What happened?'

'Because it was no use. I had to leave you behind, in the past. It was the hardest decision I've ever had to make. Each of your messages felt like tiny shards of ice splintering into my heart. I could not reply.'

She stopped and looked about for the first time.

'It's nice here. Are you happy?'

He frowned. 'How can you ask me that? How could I possibly be happy without you?'

She made as if to stand. 'I must go.'

'No, please stay, just a little longer. Tell me about your life. What happened? Your family, in England, were they kind to you? What are you doing in Paris? There's so much I want to know.'

He saw the small light in her eyes and he thought that all could not be lost.

'Would you like some tea? I have mint tea, just like from home. And music. Look I can play you music from home…' His voice drifted away.

'Thank you. Yes, my family was waiting for me when I arrived in England and everyone was very kind.'

He watched her take a deep breath.

'I got married. It happened very quickly.' The last words barely a whisper. 'Then my husband decided we should come and live here, in Paris. It was strange, coming back. Strange and so very different.' She paused, her lip was trembling. 'I missed you.'

He wanted to put his mouth on hers - still he dared not. 'Do you love him?' He blurted out the words because they had been burning his tongue since she had said, "I got married".

She changed the subject. 'Tell me, what of Ahmed? What happened to him?'

'Don't tell me you miss him too!' he half-joked.

She shook her head. 'Dear God no. Of course I don't.

He was a bad person, a thief and a liar.' She shuddered. 'Let us speak of something happier. What about you? You seem to have been very successful. When I think how you would draw all the time while we were running away. And look at you now. It is incredible.'

'You've seen my work?'

'My husband is always interested in investing in new art, so when Jean-Louis told him he had discovered a new artist - an artist with an incredible talent, my husband wanted to know more. Jean-Louis brought one of your paintings to our house.'

She gave a wry smile.

'As soon as I saw it, I knew it must be you. Then I thought it was not possible, it couldn't be...even when I saw the signature. I thought you were dead, or perhaps gone back to our homeland...'

'So, when you came to the gallery the other evening, you knew I'd be there?'

'I couldn't be sure. I dared not hope. Part of me didn't want to go. I was afraid, terrified, in fact, of seeing you again. But the other part of me, my heart and my soul, demanded to see you, just one more time - and then, when you were standing there in front of me... It was too much.'

'I couldn't believe it was you. I swore at Jean-Louis afterwards.'

He grinned, he felt happy and yet...

'Why did you marry, Layla? Why didn't you wait for me? Were you in love with this man?'

'I was alone and Nabil is a good man. Everyone likes him.'

'Rich?'

She laughed and it was the first time he had heard her laugh. 'Yes, very rich. And also very kind.'

'Does he know what you – what we all went through? Have you told him about our journey together?'

'Suleiman, there are some things that are best left by the wayside.'

'Weeds?'

She nodded.

The next days and weeks, Suleiman felt as though a burden had been lifted: he could breathe more easily, he was happy. He would draw and paint from dawn until dark, his brushes flying over the canvas; he forgot to eat; he forgot to go out; he forgot everything. Within those hours of creativity were snatched moments of passion that he had thought lost. He told himself that he had tried to resist, but after that first meeting, he offered Layla the key to his apartment.

'So you can come and go and I can see you all the time.'

'I don't know... it doesn't seem right.'

'What harm are we doing? We were meant for each other. We both know that.'

'Nabil...'

Suleiman said, 'We'll make sure he doesn't know.'

He didn't believe those words, of course, because he would make sure Nabil found out. It was the only way...

'It will not be easy for me. I may not be able to come here often.' she said.

'I don't care. I just want to be with you. You are my soul-mate, you must know that?'

She took the key.

Sometimes, he would send her a text message. 'I miss you. Can you come? Please?' Because he knew she could not refuse him; he knew she could not keep away.

Once, he asked her, 'Do you mind that I have used your father's name? On my paintings?'

She smiled softly. 'I have wondered if you would ever ask me that. No, of course not, but tell me why? Why did you?'

'It all happened so quickly. You'd gone, disappeared, and I wanted so much to be a small part of you... Somehow it seemed the right thing to do.' He slumped forward.

'Suli, it's okay. I understand. I have always understood you. And after all, what is in a name?'

'And your... husband, Nabil? Has he ever thought, wondered?'

'He has never spoken of it. So, no. Does that answer your question?'

He stood, grinning, as if suddenly released of a heavy burden. 'I shall paint your portrait! It will be the finest piece of work I have ever created.'

She sat before him, the strap of a saffron-coloured silk top slipping from her left shoulder, her right arm reaching over to catch it.

'I have told my husband that I have a surprise for him.'

He stopped his work and came over to kiss her on the mouth. 'Finally you are going to tell him the truth?'

She looked shocked. 'No, no of course not.'

'Then what?'

'My portrait of course!'

It was his turn to look shocked. 'But I'm doing this for *me* - not for another man. Besides, wouldn't he mind knowing that another man has seen you semi-naked?'

She lowered her voice. 'I have told him it is a female artist, and that it will be a very private painting to hang in his bedroom.'

'No. That can't happen. The thought of him seeing you like this…' His mouth hardened.

Each time they came together as one in the wide bed, and for those few snatched moments, it was as if they were alone in the world.

Layla had told Nabil about the surprise she was preparing for him and she knew her time was running out.

The portrait would soon be finished, and then…?

'Do you ever miss our homeland, Suleiman? Do you ever wonder what would have happened if we had stayed? I sometimes think of Moonif. Do you think he's still alive? And our family home, does someone else live there now? And what of my Baba and my sisters? I ask myself if they ever came home, but then they can't have, can they? Because I never heard.'

'You shouldn't torture yourself.'

'You haven't answered my questions.'

He sighed. 'I try never to watch the news. The destruction, the men with their guns, the dead, the children – I don't want to see that anymore.' He said. 'We should be grateful. We escaped. We were the lucky ones.'

'Are we lucky? Do you really believe that? Look at us. We are still hiding, and now I am betraying my promise to a good man. I think sometimes that I should never have listened to Moonif. I should have stayed.'

'If you had stayed then I would still be with my goats.' He looked around his bedroom. 'I'd never have had all of this and we would never have been together like we are now.'

'And Ahmed? What do you think he would have done?'

'I think he would have left anyway, but who cares?'

'Perhaps I would have followed you into the mountains.'

'Mmmm... a princess in the mountains. The goats would have had a laugh.'

She slapped his hand. 'That is unfair.'

'What of now, Layla, what of the future? What's going to happen?' He looked down at her flushed cheeks, at the fire in her eyes as he cupped her face in his hands, wanting to take her one more time.

'Your portrait – it's nearly finished.'

She pulled away from him. 'Suleiman, there is something else. Something I have not told you.'

He twirled about his fingers the dark curl that rested on her cheek, damp now from their wrestling, before pushing it away.

'No more secrets, Layla. Never again. Not now that we are together.'

'This secret is nearly three years old.'

'Tell me.'

'My secret is petite, my secret knows how to laugh. My secret is my reason for living.'

'I thought that was me?'

'You don't understand.'

'Try me.'

'I have a child. I have a daughter.'

For a few moments he said nothing: a pall of silence had fallen upon the room. No sound came from outside, no sound from anywhere. The distant view over the rooftops of the city seemed to darken.

Slowly, he stood up, took a pack of cigarettes from the table and carefully removed one. His throat felt restricted; he could think of no words.

Once more his world was falling apart. He'd been mistaken; his brain had duped him into thinking that Layla was his and his alone, and now here was the proof that he was sharing her with another man.

He put a lighter to the tip of the cigarette; he inhaled.

He couldn't bear to look at her.

He exhaled.

'I think you should leave now.'

He watched her shoulders sag.

'I think you should get dressed now and leave.' His voice hardened as he stubbed out the cigarette, crushing it into the ashtray, then pulled on his clothes.

'Listen to me, Suleiman.'

He was already at the door. 'You can leave the key on the table. Make sure you're not here by the time I get back.'

She was crying now, holding the white sheet against her amber skin; the tears were streaming down her face. 'Please, please don't go. Listen to me.'

He didn't. He went to the front door,

Chapter 24

Ahmed's journey to Paris took a lot longer than he had at first anticipated. He was constantly on the lookout for ways of acquiring money and so was, inevitably, drawn into certain circles.

He could always recognise a fellow hustler when he met one, and perhaps they saw in him the brutal determination that made him acceptable, although he never hung around long enough for his perceived aggression to be put to the test: best pocket the money and keep moving.

Caution, too, slowed him down, aware that his papers would not stand up to scrutiny.

For a while he lived with a prostitute until she kicked him out: she called him lazy and he'd laughed. Nobody had ever called him lazy before. He left all the same.

He came across other camps, other outsiders. Sometimes they would approach him and ask him for advice. He was always willing to give it, at a price: he had learned very quickly to judge a man's worth in monetary terms. His charges were high and because he had an easy-flowing tongue, those outsiders would hang on his words, as if believing their lives depended on them.

When, finally, he reached Paris he reasoned, wrongly as it turned out, that he would find Suleiman in the poorer areas, living as some paperless alien.

He took his time, found a cheap hotel - no questions asked - and began scouring the underpasses, the temporary camps that sometimes, disconcertingly, vanished overnight.

There were aliens everywhere.

He questioned them, describing Suleiman, asking if they could recall ever having seen him.

'He is my friend. He draws pictures.' His smile revealed a black tooth.

'May Allah bless you.'

There were so many…

Once, he thought he had a breakthrough: he noticed a woman pinning the drawing of a child onto the outside flap of a tent.

He moved forward.

'Nice picture. Where'd you get it?' He spoke in his own language and the woman stared at him shaking her head: he could always recognise fear when he saw it.

'The picture,' he spoke louder and reached out to touch it.

Immediately, the woman's hand was on his arm, brittle nails wanting to hurt him.

He shook her off. 'I don't want the damn thing. Just tell me where you got it?'

'Mama! Mama!' A child appeared, crying and clinging to the woman's skirt that was covered with the dust of the defeated. It was the child in the picture.

'What do you want?' The voice was threatening and it came from behind.

Ahmed turned quickly. A tall man with long dark hair woven into plaits that reached below his shoulders stood, feet firmly apart; he was not smiling.

'Who are you?'

Ahmed grinned: he recognised a fellow 'fixer' when he saw one. 'Sorry man. Sorry. I'm looking for a friend. Think he might have been this way. He was good at drawing. That looks like one of his.' He pointed to the drawing hanging on the tent. 'Perhaps you've seen him?'

The man seemed to relax. 'I might have.'

Ahmed understood. 'Five euros if you can tell me when you saw him and if you know where he went.'

'Ten.'

Ahmed sighed and nodded.

'He was here, but it was a long time ago. I remember because he was drawing all the time. He was a weirdo. He never took any money.'

'Where'd he go?'

'No idea. Think he just decided to move on.'

'Any idea where?'

'Fifteen.'

'Twelve.' His fingers played with the sharp knife in his pocket.

'He might have gone where all the tourists with money go.' The man shrugged wide shoulders.

Twelve euros exchanged hands and the child stopped crying.

Ahmed walked away from the small, rainbow-coloured tents, two dark furrows knitted neatly between his eyebrows.

Where would someone go whose only gift was the ability to draw?

He went back to his room, took out his phone and began to trawl the internet. He kicked himself hard for not having thought of it before.

After only thirty minutes of searching he found what he was looking for: he had seen enough of Suleiman's work during their long journey to recognise it immediately, although this work had more colour.

It was on the website of a Parisian art gallery. The gallery stated: 'Work by new, young artist whose work shows courage and a certain boldness infused with melancholy and subtlety of colour to make you want to admire and own each and every piece of his work'.

He noted the address.

That same evening he went to a small restaurant across the road from his hotel run by a Moroccan cook. The city air was warm and he sat outside, eating what they recommended: chicken with cumin, coriander and turmeric baked with a chilli tomato sauce and served on a bed of pearl couscous. It was a celebration.

Afterwards, he found two streetwalkers and took them back to his room and spent an enjoyable night, floating between the two bodies.

Next morning he kicked them out after paying them for their services, then he went and used the shower at the end of the corridor, humming to himself as he rubbed away the perfume of the night's exertions. 'I have found my friend.'

And his grin stretched the width of his face.

It was mid-morning, on a grey day with low-hanging

cloud, by the time he found the gallery in the small cobbled street.

Peering through one of the wide windows on either side of the entrance door, he saw a man seated on a small leather sofa, his legs crossed, speaking on a phone. The man had fair hair that was tied back from his face.

Two pieces of Suleiman's work were on display in each window; both were perched on easels.

He stared hard at one of the paintings; it was of a girl sitting in a rattan chair, dark curls falling across her shoulders as she gazed over a burning landscape.

'Layla,' he whispered under his breath.

Shame on her! Shame on them both.

Then he noticed the figure standing behind her in the shadows; the face was obscured. He wondered, was it supposed to be Suleiman, or was it him, Ahmed?

He turned about, crossed the road and entered a café opposite. He ordered a sandwich and a coffee and sat back to watch - and wait.

It was some time before he saw Suleiman arrive and enter the gallery. He would have been forgiven for not immediately recognising his friend: Suleiman was wearing a pale blue cotton jacket over a black shirt, designer jeans and tan-coloured shoes. A black carry-case was slung over his shoulder.

My friend, you have changed.

Ahmed stood up and was about to move when Suleiman re-emerged almost immediately. He was talking animatedly with the man he had seen sitting on the sofa. They were laughing. Laughing? It wasn't right.

Then the other man turned and locked the door; he linked arms with Suleiman and they walked away:

friends.

Ahmed did not go back there for a couple of days. It took him a while to sift through and try to analyse what he had seen.

He didn't understand.

It hurt him that Suleiman had never laughed like that with him, had never allowed him, Ahmed, to link arms like that.

He felt angry, disappointed.

When, finally, he made up his mind to go back, he arrived just as Suleiman was leaving the gallery. Only this time he was on his own.

Ahmed followed him along the street and down into the throat of the Metro.

The journey was short, but Ahmed had time to observe Suleiman from a distance: to notice how happy Suleiman seemed; how he frequently smiled to himself, shaking his head as if at some private joke. He saw how free and confident Suleiman seemed; holding his head high, his shoulders back. He saw how Suleiman had changed.

Back out in the open air, Ahmed shadowed Suleiman along several streets; saw him pop into a *charcuterie* and come out with a small bag of provisions, then saunter down the Avenue de Breteuil, across the Boulevard Garibaldi until they reached Avenue Emile Zola.

Suleiman stopped at number thirty-five.

Ahmed whistled softly, as he saw Suleiman push a side button before going through two large green doors, and step into what looked like an inner courtyard.

Ahmed stood for a few minutes on the corner of the

street, watching and waiting.

'I think it's time we met up, my friend. I have something to show you that will wipe that stupid grin off your face.'

He saw the shutters on one of the upper-floor apartments being flung open and Suleiman appeared, leaning over a worn balustrade, waving and, instinctively, Ahmed put up his hand to wave back.

Then he saw a young woman walking quickly on the other side of the street. She, too, was waving. He could not see her face: it was turned away from him.

Suleiman disappeared from view and the shutters were closed once more as the woman stepped into that inner courtyard.

Five minutes passed. Then half an hour, one hour, two hours. He had smoked almost all of his cigarettes when the heavy green doors opened and the young woman stepped out into the street. She stood for a moment, looking carefully up and down, and then she turned and hurried away.

Ahmed stared at her departing figure, seeing then what his eyes had been telling him all along, seeing what he had not thought possible.

Layla!

So, she wasn't in England, she was here, in Paris. And she was seeing Suleiman.

Without thinking, he hurried after her, listening to her footsteps ringing on the pavement opposite, as if her feet wanted to dance.

There was the usual traffic jam, and a bus halted and for a moment blocked his view, but it didn't take him long to catch up with her.

She had stopped and was speaking on her phone, then she put the phone back in her bag and stood waiting.

He watched.

A moment later, a chauffeur-driven black Mercedes with tinted windows drew up alongside her, the chauffeur got out and opened one of the doors and she climbed into the back seat.

He saw that she hadn't changed that much, perhaps more beautiful now. A cluster of dark curls encircled her head; she was taller than he remembered.

Ahmed watched the car pull away. There was a familiar tightening in his chest. So the two of them had found each other again? And he had been left out?

He felt his shoulders sag.

Chapter 25

It was the first time they had met for over a week, despite numerous messages from Layla, begging him to at least speak to her.

In the end, Suleiman knew he had to see her again.

'Does she look like you?'

'She looks a lot like her father.'

'What's her name?'

'Elena. It was my mother's name. Suleiman…'

'How old?'

'You're not listening to me. The child is not my husband's. He thinks… I told him…' The words spilled out. 'I told him that I was raped. He is a good man and he wanted to protect me. He accepted to marry me, to take care of the child. I had no other option.'

'Raped? But … when? Was it when you got to England? I should have been with you. You needed my protection.' He slapped his forehead hard. 'My God, this is all my fault.'

'Suleiman.' Her slim hand with its golden wedding band touched his arm. Her smile was soft, it had lost the scornfulness he had often seen before. 'I was taken it is true, but the man who did that to me, I loved him and I think he loved me.'

He stared at her; his brain was struggling to assemble the jigsaw pieces in the right order. His stomach churned.

He asked, 'Do you have any other children?'

'We have never made love. My husband has a preference for young men. He just wants me to be at his side, like a valuable and expensive possession. And to behave honourably. To him honour is more important than anything.'

'What are you saying, Layla?'

'In my own way I love my husband for what he has done for me. For the way he adores my daughter. I promised always to behave with honour. And then you walked back into my life and I dropped my guard and now...'

'The child,' he paused a moment, hardly daring to ask the question. 'Is she mine?'

Layla nodded.

'I have a daughter.' He sat back on the wide sofa, his arm around her shoulders as he repeated the words over and over. 'I have a daughter. Elena. A daughter.'

He turned to her. 'You must divorce him. Come away with me, you and Elena. Please. We can't continue like this. Not any more. I want you with me forever. I have money now.'

'Don't you see, Suleiman, that it is impossible? That would bring dishonour, to him and to my family. He doesn't deserve that, none of them do. Besides, he'd look for me, I'm sure. And he would kill you.'

'I don't care. Nothing matters. I will do anything. We were meant to be together.'

'Suli.'

As she spoke he smiled to himself: no one else ever shortened his name; it filled him with the sudden warmth of hope.

'Suli, I have always loved you. I will never stop loving you. But you must understand that what you are asking is ... it is impossible.'

'Nothing is impossible Layla. Tell him the truth. Explain to him... He is a man of the world. Tell him I am Elena's father. Tell him I never meant to lose you. Tell him that I love you and you love me. Ask him to set you free. If he is as good as you say, surely he'd do this for you?'

He paused. 'When can I see my daughter?'

'The truth is like a knife Suleiman. It can kill too.'

Chapter 26

Suleiman was coming out of the shower when the doorbell rang.

The day, the afternoon, the precise moment when all his happiness dropped into the abyss.

The day, the afternoon, the precise moment when Allah pointed a finger at him.

He put on a soft, white bathrobe, tied the belt with precision as the doorbell jangled again as if someone were leaning on it and would not let go.

She was early. Perhaps there was a problem?

For a few seconds he stood back holding the door, conscious that his lips were slightly parted as he searched for his words. Ahmed?

'You? How…? What are you doing here? How'd you find me?'

'Bastard!' The word was spoken in a familiar tone. 'It's been a while, hasn't it? Why'd you run away from me all that time ago? After all we'd been through together.' Ahmed grinned as he peered over Suleiman's shoulder.

'Aren't you going to ask me in, or did I interrupt

something?'

'Why? Why are you here? I don't understand. What do you want?'

'Mind if I come in? Sit down maybe? You know, as you would welcome an old friend. Because we are very old friends, aren't we?'

Ahmed pushed passed Suleiman and padded forward, turning his head this way and that, taking in the polished floor, the white marble bust of a woman, the deep leather sofa covered with scatter cushions.

He inhaled the perfumed air of the candles burning cinnamon and frankincense.

'Nice place.'

He noted the partially-closed voile curtains wafting in the outside, gentle breeze.

He noted the delicate cups and saucers carefully set out on the low Chinese coffee table and the baklava pastries.

'Come on, smile! Aren't you at least a little bit pleased to see me, my friend? We were business partners once, remember? Perhaps I'm not good enough for you now?'

'I'm expecting someone. You can't stay.' A hesitation, 'We could meet up. Later.'

Ahmed went and sat on the sofa, spreading his legs out over the polished floor and clasping his hands behind his head. He gestured to the cups and saucers. 'Aren't you going to offer me a drink?'

'It'll have to be quick.'

'Whisky, then?'

'Ice?'

'Nah. As it comes.'

'How'd you find me?'

'I have my ways.'

Suleiman felt a shudder slip down his spine as Ahmed tapped the side of his nose. He wondered why it was that Ahmed seemed to carry with him a darkness he could never understand,

"Sides, that little waitress, what was her name? Remember her? She put me on the right road. Enjoyed a spicy couple of hours with her. You've always had good taste, my man.'

Suleiman shrank back as if Ahmed had hit him and Ahmed saw Suleiman's face, and he knew Suleiman was thinking what he wanted him to think.

He hadn't done anything to the girl, except put a hand up her skirt which, in his head, she should have enjoyed. He hadn't gone any further. She'd cried. He'd seen a lot of people cry over the past few years and he had very little compassion left, if he'd ever had any at all, that is. But she was pretty. He could have done anything he liked with her and that was the point: he had the power and he hadn't used it. He'd felt good about that. He'd forced her to lie down beside him; he'd put his arm around her shoulders, holding her close, feeling her sobs as her breasts heaved up and down, wiping the tears on her cheeks with his tee-shirt; he'd even remembered a song from his childhood and he'd hummed it to her; he hadn't thought she liked it, so he'd stopped.

'Cécile, wasn't it? She liked you. Said she thought you'd gone to Paris. I sort of wheedled that bit out of her. She wasn't that chatty. Nice body though. Delightfully plump.'

He took a gulp of whisky. 'Did you know that back

home, when an unmarried man has sex with an unmarried woman he's given one hundred lashes? Did you know that? You're lucky we're here, otherwise we'd both be nursing our wounds. And you'd be getting at least five hundred lashes!'

'I've no idea what you're talking about. Think it's time you left.'

Even though Ahmed felt a deep-seated hatred towards Suleiman, he still wanted his friendship.

Ever since their first meeting in the schoolyard all that time ago, he had watched the way Suleiman smiled at others and he'd wanted Suleiman to look at him like that, to give him that special smile. It seemed, though, that each time he offered his hand in friendship, Suleiman turned away from him, calling him a people smuggler and a thief. That hurt: it hurt like a cramp in his gut, and it would not go away.

Still, he was willing to give it one more try.

'It is you, my friend, who have a problem. A very big problem.' His tone hardened. 'You don't know me, not really *know* me! You've always treated me like something bad on the bottom of your shoe. I did my best to get us over here. Even you must agree that without me you'd never have made it.'

Suleiman spoke through a tightened jaw. 'I don't know why you're here or what you want, but…'

'My friend!' Ahmed clapped his hands into the air. 'We are still friends, aren't we? I've been thinking… in fact I've thought a lot about you. You've come a long way since sending all those people off to die.'

The air in the room hung heavy; he watched Suleiman move to open the window wider, heard his sharp intake of breath.

'I never sent anyone off to die. Never.'

'Nah! Who you trying to kid? You just took their money and turned your back. No worries, my friend. I'm not here to judge. As I said, I've been thinking a lot about you. I think you need a new business partner.'

'Business partner? I don't think so! I especially don't need you. And for God's sake stop calling me your friend. I am not your friend. I have never been your friend. You're just a…"

'Perhaps I could help you change your mind?'

'Finish your drink then get out.'

'You always thought you were better than me, didn't you? You've always looked down on me, you and that rich bitch we dragged around everywhere. Thanks to her we could've been killed.'

'Thanks to her we made it here. Thanks to her money, remember? Now get out.'

'One minute, my friend. I have not finished.'

'I am not your friend! I have never been your friend! When will you ever get that through your thick skull?'

'Even so,' the tone changed. 'I think I could make you change your mind. I have information…' Ahmed tapped his nose. 'You said you were expecting someone? Think I can make a wild guess. This someone's been here several times, hasn't she? I've been watching your place. In the interests of getting to know you better, you understand?'

Suleiman recognised the destructive laugh.

'You see, I've seen her. I've even noticed how she gives her driver the slip: being dropped off further down the street, outside one of those smart shops. To me, that doesn't seem very honest, now does it? For a married woman that is. Because she is married, isn't she?'

Suleiman felt his breath sucked out of his body; his fingers folded into a tight fist. 'You been spying on me? How long...?'

'How long? Put it this way, how many times she been here? She always stays for ... let me see,' he extracted a small notepad from his jacket pocket.

He licked a finger as he consulted the blank pages, taking his time.

'I suppose it averages out, a couple of hours twice a week – if it can be arranged. I mean, because she has a child. A daughter. You do know that, don't you? I'll bet you do. I've done my homework. Your visitor stays on average between forty-five minutes and a couple of hours, if you're lucky,' he grinned. 'Very lucky that is. Then she leaves. When she leaves here she is smiling; she almost skips down the street. I often wonder what she tells the chauffeur. Does she give him money to keep his mouth shut, or does she straddle him in the front seat as alternative payment.'

Suleiman was across the room and onto Ahmed as the last words left his mouth.

The tumbler containing the whisky fell to the floor, spilling what was left, smashing the cut-glass.

His fingers reached out to grab at Ahmed's neck but Ahmed was more agile and he slipped, laughing, from Suleiman's grasp.

They fell on each other, rolling over and over like dogs, although this time one of them had in his mind to erase the other from the face of the earth.

Ahmed crawled towards the door, blood pouring from

his nose and his ear.

'You'll be sorry. You'll be sorry for this, my friend.' His laugh was ugly because it was sad and he was unable to hold back the tears.

'Just wait and you'll see. And that woman you thought you'd saved, Nadia, she never made it. Did you know that? Did nobody tell you? She and the kid, they drowned. Your fault. It was you who put them into that boat, my friend. Your fault!' He screamed again as he stood, holding on to the wall, 'It's all your damned fault! You went against the will of Allah, my friend!'

'Shut it! Shut your face. Shut it!' Suleiman prayed that would be last time he ever heard those two words as he wondered once again when it was that Ahmed had found God.

Minutes later, Ahmed stood outside on the pavement, looking up at Suleiman's apartment.

Opposite the apartment was a small square with trees and gardens where children were playing. The late afternoon air was still warm. He could hear their shrieks of laughter; he could see the mothers sitting on the stone benches chatting.

He wiped a hand across his bloodied face.

Suleiman stood staring at the door he had slammed shut with all the force he could muster, as he screamed, 'Get out! Get out!'

He waited a moment or two, thinking that Ahmed would come back; that perhaps he would fling the door open like some bad djinni.

He put his ear to the door and listened. Silence. He opened it slowly but there was no-one. No Ahmed standing at the top of the stairs.

He closed the door and moved back inside.

He went and sat down on the sofa where Ahmed had been sitting only moments ago. He was trembling. He looked down at his hand: it was covered in blood: Ahmed's blood.

He closed his eyes as he remembered Ahmed's words. So, Nadia and her child had drowned? That couldn't be right – could it? He'd made sure they were safe, hadn't he? He remembered sending up prayers for them. He'd even stood and watched the boat vanish on the horizon.

It was a dinghy…

The doorbell rang again. Suleiman stiffened. Then a knocking.

'What has happened to you? To your face? Who did this?' Layla gasped as she stood in the doorway looking at Suleiman. 'And your hand! What have you done?'

He told her. He told her everything.

They sat together, holding each other.

'He's been looking for me, Layla. He's been looking for both of us.'

'How did he find us?'

'I don't know.'

'You didn't tell him…?' her face blanched.

'I didn't have to tell him. He guessed.'

'Guessed? But how could he? What did you say?' She began to cry.

He reached out and wiped her tears with his finger. 'I swear to you I didn't say anything. He's been watching us.'

'I should go. If he comes back…'

'He was shouting. He was angry. I don't think I've ever seen him that angry – at least not against me.'

'What was he shouting?'

'He kept on saying, "it's all your damned fault, you went against the will of Allah". I don't know what he meant. And why would I do that?'

'Suleiman, did you tell him I was married?'

'Of course not. But I keep telling you. He knows. He knew already.' He felt her panic rising.

'But, Nabil… he mustn't find out! Oh, dear God! How can this be happening? If Nabil finds out…'

He wasn't listening. He straightened up. 'We must leave. Go away. Now, this instant. Together. I'll leave a note for Jean-Louis; he'll understand.' He stood up. 'You won't need any baggage, we can buy whatever we need on the way…'

She shook her head. 'I can't. Not like this. It is wrong. And you are forgetting I have daughter – we have a daughter. I cannot leave her behind, Suli'.'

'We'll come back for her. Later.'

She shook her head. 'No.'

'But once we're free, we can have more daughters, more sons.'

She put a finger on his lips. 'Please do not force me. I should go now.'

'But you'll come back?'

'First let us wait. Let us wait and see what Ahmed has planned. He is capable of doing bad things. We both know that.'

Chapter 27

That night, an envelope is thrust under the door of his apartment. Suleiman is still sitting on the sofa.

He cannot drive Ahmed's words out of his head.

He is afraid.

He goes to the door, bends down and picks up the envelope.

He holds it in his hand as if weighing its contents; the envelope is smudged with dirt and there are water marks.

He sees that it has already been opened by someone else.

It has been read by someone else.

Ahmed's words swirl around in his head: "You went against the will of Allah." He shudders.

He goes back to the door and goes to look down the wide staircase: there is no-one. He hears the street door below bang loudly.

He goes back inside and falls onto the sofa, turning the envelope over and over. His slim hands shake. He stares at the words covered in grime, but still visible on the envelope: *For my daughters.* He feels his heart give a flutter – not in a good way.

With great care, he peers inside the envelope but he does not remove the content from its protective surroundings.

Then he closes his eyes and allows two sheets of slim paper to slip out into his hands.

He opens his eyes again, and he begins to read.

My darling daughters: In the name of God, the Merciful, the Compassionate, if you are reading this it will be because I am no longer able to protect you.

My dear children, lies have been spread about me, but I swear to you as God is my witness that I have always tried to follow a just and righteous path.

Your dear mother and you, my children, have always been more precious to me than life itself. Once, and only once, did I commit a crime so shocking that my tears are still heavy with remorse. Perhaps, then, it is right that I should now be punished.

Suleiman does not want to read any further.

The letter is not meant for him.

He knows that it is meant for Layla.

Still, he continues to hold it, imagining the paper wet with the author's tears; he sees the elegant fingers so often described to him by Layla, the fingers that held the pen and wrote this note, the hand that once held a violin when the final notes were discordant.

I confess to you my children, that I forced your mother to give away a piece of her own flesh and it was if I had cut out a piece of her heart.

In my weakness I could not accept that another man had forced his seed into my beautiful wife and it is only now, now that the devil searches for me, that I ask forgiveness not from your mother, because she is no longer with us, but from that child – now a man – the child I never knew, the child I forced her to reject because I could not bear the thought that another had taken her by force.

When that baby emerged from her body he did not cry; not a single tear. I thought then that he must be cursed, I know now that the curse was on me.

I swear to you I tried to find the imam to whom I gave that baby and who was sworn to secrecy, but I left it too late and he is no longer on this earth.

When the imam left with the silent bundle, my conscience spoke to me, and I whispered to him that the child should be called Suleiman.

I have carried this guilt with me for so many years and I know that soon they will come for me.

I have asked Moonif to give you this letter should anything happen to me, and to take care of you and make sure you get to England.

Do not forget my darling daughters that you have a brother somewhere on this vast earth whom you may never know.

Forgive me. Allah is great.
Your devoted father,
Yusuf Abadi.

What had she said to him? "The truth is like a knife Suleiman. It can kill too."

Chapter 28

Piercing his lips Suleiman blows into the night air, and a fine column of cold breath funnels out of his mouth and wafts out into darkness.

After reading the letter he had walked out into the night, wandering the streets confused, angry. Disbelieving. Remembering. Was it possible? What was it Ahmed had said? Something about, when a man copulates with a woman outside marriage, they get one hundred lashes.

But a sister? And a married woman? What then?

He feels the bile rise again into his throat and he swallows it back.

He wishes he could speak with the imam, the man who once told him: 'God is with you wherever you are; and He sees the things that you do.'

But if God was with him, surely he should have warned him, found a way to tell him...

So, it was true, he was indeed cursed.

His world was crumbling, and this time it wasn't Ahmed's fault, was it?

Layla, Layla, Layla.

He thinks he can hear music. Is someone playing the oud? It is soft, distanced.

He can see no one but then he is not really looking. It is music from his homeland. Warmth. The mountains, the goats. Drawing in peace. The imam.

It is what his life could have been.

Somehow he has reached a bridge, he leans over the cold, white stone and looks down at the city's lights reflected in the freezing river below.

He slaps gloveless hands over his forearms: it is cold. He has known colder.

A gust of bitter wind blows a solitary raindrop from the dark branches of the trees that line the quay below.

A pleasure boat glides past in the dark; coloured lanterns hang from wires that stretch around the boat swaying and illuminating the deck, glittering reflections thrown down onto the dark, silent water. There is the sound of laughter, the clinking of glasses, a band plays.

He wonders if the water is deep.

He takes off his coat and folds it carefully.

He bends down to remove his shoes: they are expensive.

He looks at his watch: nearly ten o'clock. He hesitates, starts to undo the gold strap, changes his mind: the watch stays.

The boat disappears below the bridge, taking with it the laughter and the fleeting sounds of happiness.

He takes a deep breath. He has come all this way. Why? For what?

He has betrayed people: his mother who wasn't his mother and his father who wasn't his father, but who had told him the truth.

So, this is his punishment.

Surely, though, he was the one who had been betrayed? Deprived of a mother who would surely have loved him, sisters?

One sister...

He thinks he hears someone shout as he climbs onto the top of the stone parapet and looks down.

He slips a hand into his pocket and takes out his last and final drawing of Layla: she is smiling at him, but his fingers are cold and it slips from their hold. He screams and reaches out. Too late. The picture floats down, down into the darkness below.

He thinks he hears the same voice call out again, 'My friend!'

What friend?

The voice is familiar.

He thinks he hears the sound of running feet.

He knows it is too late and they are too far away.

Now that it is over and he can think more clearly, he wonders when it was that everything changed.

When was it that he had looked at Layla differently?

Was it at that first detention centre, where they had been forced to stay a while before climbing through a broken fence, to find the road to wherever it was they were going? The road to nowhere?

Was it after that first shower, when Ahmed had emerged clean-shaven for once, hostile eyes beneath thick eyebrows and he, Suleiman, had seen how Layla had stared with surprise at Ahmed?

She was so very beautiful, he thought his heart would break into a thousand pieces with longing for her.

Sometimes, when she turned to smile at him, he saw

her eyes light up.

Layla.

If only we had known….

Tears begin to trickle down his cheeks and he finds he cannot stop them. He is crying!

The water feels cold; colder than anything he has ever known.

Down, down he goes as his fingers and toes turn to ice.

Then he remembers the boat capsizing and Ahmed holding on to Layla, holding her in his arms and she staring at him, as the water went over their heads.

He flounders once more, then stops.

It had all been for nothing after all.

One more time, Ahmed shouts, 'My friend!'

That night Layla tells her husband the truth.

He roars with pain like the bear he is and he growls that she has betrayed him. She must go. He will not allow her to take their daughter.

She goes to find Suleiman with a small suitcase and the news that she is expecting their second child.

She cannot find him. He is not at home.

Chapter 29

'Put those over there, mate, okay?'

Ahmed carried the heavy box and put it at the back of the room. He looked around and sighed. 'So many boxes,' he said.

'They won't be here long. Someone's going to be asking for help soon.'

The phone rang. 'Told you!' The other man walked over to a desk and picked up the phone. 'Yeah, yeah. Fine. We'll organise it. Ahmed will. All right with you Ahmed? That's another load arrived since last night! Crazy!'

'Where are they from this time?'

'Who knows, but they're in Calais now and they need you to go and help translate.'

Ahmed nodded. 'Fine with me. What else do they need?'

'Baby clothes. Can you imagine? Baby clothes! I mean, who'd take their kids on that sort of a journey? Putting your kids in those plastic boats. Honestly, I don't understand…'

'They're not boats.'

'What?'

'They're not boats, they're dinghies.'

'Okay, whatever. Tell you what, if I was a dad I'd never do that to my kid.'

'When do I leave?'

'Tomorrow morning, first thing. We'll load up tonight.' The man, whose name was Bruno, shook his head. 'Apparently they've got one baby just over three months' old and a couple of five-year olds. They need nappies, kiddie's clothes, shoes. We had a big donation arrive yesterday, so that should be okay.'

'Did their mother survive?'

'No idea. Didn't ask. Still, she should have known better.'

Ahmed watched as Bruno went over to check the boxes, still shaking his head and muttering: 'Unbelievable'.

'Give me a few minutes.' He went outside and lit a cigarette.

He bent a knee and leant against the wall. He inhaled deeply.

With closed eyes he saw the refugees trying to escape in their dinghies. He understood their despair, their fear.

What did someone like Bruno know?

How could he ever know what it was like to run away, to be always hungry, always looking over your shoulder?

What did he know about trying to survive and handing over all your money to a people smuggler who'd load dozens of you onto one poxy inflatable, or shove you onto a waiting lorry?

He shuddered: it was the guilt. It never went away.

He missed Suleiman. After all they'd been through

together, he'd never thought... never imagined... All he'd ever wanted was for Suleiman to like him. Why couldn't he have done that? Just once? Just a little? And Layla? He'd always known she could never love him, but why couldn't she have smiled at him the way she smiled at Suleiman?

When he'd arrived at the bridge and seen Suleiman standing there on top of one of the stone arches, his heart had leapt into his mouth. He wasn't able to breathe, it was as if all the air had been sucked out of his body.

He'd started to run as fast as he could, shouting as he ran, 'My friend! My friend!'

Too late.

He could still hear the splash as Suleiman's body hit the water. He'd jumped after him into the dark, fast-flowing waters but he couldn't find him, couldn't find his friend. The water was cold, so very cold. He dived down again and again, his clothes clung to him like weights and in the end he was forced to give up.

Some people had gathered at the water's edge.

Someone dragged him out of the water.

Someone went to get a blanket, someone else brought him a hot drink.

He sobbed bitter tears.

They took him to a small building nearby where they sat him down.

'Where do you live?' They asked, their voices anxious.

'Where will you sleep?'

They knew, of course. They understood. They offered him a bed for the night. They found more blankets and some dry clothes and he slept in that small place.

A priest came by. Ahmed said he was not of that religion. The priest said it didn't matter, that he would pray for him anyway. And Ahmed thought that nobody had ever prayed for him before.

'How you doin'?' Bruno had come out to join him: he looked anxious.

'I'm fine.' Ahmed looked at the other man: a man of average height and build, with long hair and a big laugh. The man who had pulled him out of the dark waters.

'Do you fancy a drink later? Or a bite to eat? Really sorry if I upset you just now. Sometimes I put my foot into my mouth. I don't know what happens.'

'No worries. I've heard worse.'

'Can I ask you something?'

'Sure.' Ahmed dropped his cigarette onto the ground and crushed it with his cowboy boot.

'It's just that when you first offered to help out here, I didn't believe you. I thought you were after something. It happens a lot, you know? But you're not like that, are you? No, honest, I've never met anyone like you, someone who's been through… well, anyway, you know what I mean. I just never imagined you'd want to stay and help.'

Ahmed looked away. 'You don't know me,' he said.

'Yeah, but you really do care about these people, don't you?'

'Maybe…'

'I can see it in your face. You care for them. You spend time with them. You translate for them and even if you don't speak their language, you sit with them. I've seen you holding their hands! You're never in a hurry…'

'Shut it, Bruno! I'm no saint!' He gave a sarcastic laugh. 'Not by a long way.'

'No, I understand that but… can I ask you something? Swear you won't mind.'

"Course I won't mind. You saved my life, remember?'

'That was nothing. I just happened to be there. But, you see, I've never had a friend. A real friend.' Bruno stopped. He looked embarrassed and took a step back as Ahmed moved forward.

Ahmed thumped him on the shoulder, and then Ahmed grinned with a grin that split his face from ear to ear and he said, 'My friend.'

He paused a moment and in his mind a door closed and a key turned in its lock, then the key fell into the muddy waters below and then it was gone.

'My friend,' he said again, and he smiled at Bruno with a happiness he had never before known.

THE END